S0-ADP-411

JOIN THE FUN
IN CABIN SIX . . .

KATIE is the perfect team player She loves competitive games, planned activities, and coming up with her own great ideas.

MEGAN would rather lose herself in fantasyland than get into organized fun.

SARAH would be much happier if she could spend her time reading instead of exerting herself.

ERIN is much more interested in boys, clothes, and makeup than in playing kids' games at camp.

TRINA hates conflicts. She just wants everyone to be happy . . .

AND THEY ARE! Despite all their differences, the Cabin Six bunch are having the time of their lives at CAMP SUNNYSIDE!

Look for More Fun and Games with
CAMP SUNNYSIDE FRIENDS
by Marilyn Kaye
from Avon Books

MARILYN KAYE is the author of many popular books for young readers, including the "Out of This World" series and the "Sisters" books. She is an associate professor at St. John's University and lives in Brooklyn, New York.

Camp Sunnyside is the camp Marilyn wishes that she had gone to every summer when she was a kid.

Avon Books are available at special quantity discounts for bulk purchases for sales promotions, premiums, fund raising or educational use. Special books, or book excerpts, can also be created to fit specific needs.

For details write or telephone the office of the Director of Special Markets, Avon Books, Dept. FP, 1350 Avenue of the Americas, New York, New York 10019, 1-800-238-0658.

Balancing Act

Marilyn Kaye

AN AVON CAMELOT BOOK

If you purchased this book without a cover, you should be aware that
this book is stolen property. It was reported as "unsold and destroyed"
to the publisher, and neither the author nor the publisher has received
any payment for this "stripped book."

CAMP SUNNYSIDE FRIENDS #18: BALANCING ACT is an original pub-
lication of Avon Books. This work has never before appeared in book form.

AVON BOOKS
A division of
The Hearst Corporation
1350 Avenue of the Americas
New York, New York 10019

Copyright © 1992 by Marilyn Kaye
Published by arrangement with the author
Library of Congress Catalog Card Number: 92-90003
ISBN: 0-380-76918-2
RL: 5.2

All rights reserved, which includes the right to reproduce this book or portions
thereof in any form whatsoever except as provided by the U.S. Copyright Law.
For information address Writers House Inc., 21 West 26 Street, New York,
New York 10010.

First Avon Camelot Printing: July 1992

CAMELOT TRADEMARK REG. U.S. PAT. OFF. AND IN OTHER COUNTRIES, MARCA
REGISTRADA, HECHO EN U.S.A.

Printed in the U.S.A.

OPM   10 9 8 7 6 5 4 3 2 1

For Phil Clark

Balancing Act

Chapter 1

Megan Lindsay sat on her bottom bunk bed in cabin six and placed playing cards down on the spread. Fingering a lock of red hair, she gazed at the cards with a slight frown and tried to remember how to play solitaire. Then she let out a long, deep sigh. Solitaire was not her favorite game in the world. And when the skies outside were gray and cloudy, free period wasn't her favorite time of day at Camp Sunnyside.

Her eyes roamed the cabin. Directly across from her, Trina Sandburg was perched up on a pillow. Her sweet, serious face with its neat cap of brown hair was bent over a pad of paper. She was scribbling furiously.

Probably writing a letter home, Megan thought. That was what Trina always did during gloomy free periods.

Above Trina, Katie Dillon lay flat on her

back, a headset clamped to her head. Her eyes were closed, and Megan would have thought she was sleeping except for the fact that her feet were twitching in time to the music blasting into her ears.

At the far end of the cabin, on the only single bed, Erin Chapman's long blonde hair concealed her face as she examined her hands. Megan watched for a moment as Erin carefully applied a bright pink color to her fingernails. It wasn't a very interesting sight, especially since Megan saw her doing this almost daily.

Megan couldn't see the girl on the bunk above her, but she didn't have to. She knew exactly what Sarah Fine was doing right that minute. She was curled up with a book.

Megan grimaced. Here they were, with an hour of free time to do anything they wanted to do, and nobody was doing anything interesting. "Anyone want to play tennis?" she asked without much hope. Tennis was her personal passion. Nobody else in cabin six liked to play. So she wasn't surprised when her question got no response.

She tried again. "You guys want to take canoes out on the lake?"

At least this suggestion got some reaction.

Trina's eyes didn't leave her pad but she murmured, "It looks like it's going to rain, Megan."

"But it might not," Megan argued. Even so, looking out the window, she knew Trina was probably right. "Okay, maybe it's not a good time to be out on the lake. We could see what's going on over at arts and crafts. Or wait, I've got a better idea! Ping-pong! Let's go over to the Activities Hall, and . . ." Her voice trailed off as she realized that not one of the girls was even listening to her.

This is so annoying, she thought. She slid off her bed, got down on the floor, and began rummaging under her bed. She had to search for a while, but she finally found what she was looking for—a roll of caps, left over from a skit the girls had put on weeks ago. She placed them on the floor. And then she stomped hard.

With satisfaction, she observed the reactions to the loud bang. Trina's head jerked up. From above, Sarah let out a shriek. Even Katie pulled off her headset.

Carolyn, their counselor, flew out of her private room. "What was that?"

"I stepped on some caps," Megan replied.

Carolyn stared at her in bewilderment. "What did you do that for?"

"To get everyone's attention."

"Well, you got it," Erin growled. "And you made me mess up my nails. What's the matter with you, Megan?"

"What's the matter with *you?*" Megan countered. *"All* of you!"

Sarah leaned over the side of her bed. Behind her glasses, her eyes were puzzled. "What are you talking about?"

Megan put her hands on her hips. "It's free period, and we're not doing anything interesting."

"What's wrong with that?" Katie asked.

Carolyn nodded. "Megan, maybe everyone just wants a little quiet time." She yawned. "I know *I'd* appreciate that."

"Sorry," Megan said. "But it just doesn't seem right to me. Here we are, at the best summer camp in the whole wide world. Can't we find something better to do than just hang around in the cabin?"

Erin gave her a withering look. "How do you know this is the best summer camp in the whole wide world? You've never been to any other one."

Megan ignored that. "There are a zillion things we could be doing, and we're not taking advantage of them."

"Like what?" Trina asked.

4

"Swimming! Horseback riding! Hiking!"

Katie rolled her eyes. "You talk like that's something special. We do that stuff every day."

Erin waved her hands in the air to dry her nails. "You know where I wish I was right now? Italy."

Trina sighed. Katie's eyes became glazed over. Looking up, Megan saw a dreamy smile on Sarah's face. Megan couldn't blame them. Her own thoughts went back to April, when the cabin six girls had all gone to Italy for their spring holiday. Everything about Italy, from the ancient buildings to the special ice cream, was new and amazing to them.

"Italy was super," she admitted.

"No kidding," Katie remarked. "Compared to Italy, Sunnyside seems so . . . ordinary."

"That's because we've been coming here every summer for four years," Megan said. "If we went to Italy every year, it wouldn't seem so special either."

"I doubt that," Erin snorted.

"I think Megan's making a good point," Carolyn told the others. "When you get used to a place, it doesn't seem quite so extraordinary anymore. Like our own homes, for example. I'll bet there are many people who would be thrilled to live in nice homes, the way we all do. But we

5

probably don't think about that. We take what we have for granted."

"Exactly!" Megan declared. She gazed at Carolyn, pleased that she had described the problem so well. "We don't appreciate Camp Sunnyside anymore."

"I guess you're right," Sarah said. "But what can we do about that?"

Megan considered the problem. "Well, we could pretend this is the first day of our first summer, and treat every activity like it's something new. How about it?"

The expressions that greeted this idea were less than enthusiastic. At least Trina was kind. "You might be able to do that, Megan, because you've got so much imagination. But I don't think the rest of us are that good at pretending."

Megan looked around at her cabin mates. Every one of them looked bored. Something had to be done about this, she decided, or the rest of the summer was going to be pretty dreary. These girls needed a push. If only Megan could think of something to push them *with*.

The dining hall was in its usual state of commotion as campers scurried about with their dinner trays. The cabin six girls joined the line to get food.

Sarah straightened her glasses and peered at the girls going by with trays. "What are we having? Can anyone see?"

"It looks like chicken pie," Katie announced.

"Oh, okay."

Megan turned to Sarah. "Hey, I thought you *liked* chicken pie."

Sarah shrugged. "Sure, I like chicken pie."

"Well, you certainly don't sound very happy about it."

"What do you want me to do?" Sarah asked. "Jump up and down? Pretend I've never eaten chicken pie before?"

Katie thrust a hand dramatically over her heart. "Chicken pie! A brand new amazing experience!"

Megan uttered a silent groan. Was there nothing that could get her cabin mates excited? The girls collected their trays and settled down at their usual table. They had just begun eating when Ms. Winkle, the camp director, went to the front of the room.

"Could I have everyone's attention for the evening announcements?" she called out.

The noise in the dining hall softened a little. At Megan's table, the girls turned their heads

7

toward Ms. Winkle, but nobody seemed terribly curious. Ms. Winkle's evening announcements were pretty predictable. They usually had to do with a movie on the lake, or an upcoming camp-fire. Ms. Winkle always looked distracted. But Megan thought that this particular evening the camp director seemed more flustered than usual. "Girls, please! This is important!"

The room actually became quiet. "I have some very interesting news for you," Ms. Winkle said. "In a few days, Camp Sunnyside will be enter-taining some very special visitors."

Megan watched Erin's eyes light up, and she could read her mind. Whoever these visitors were, Erin would be very pleased if they were male.

Ms. Winkle continued. "Now, I'm sure you're aware of the One World Games, which are being held in a few weeks in upstate New York. Teams from all over the world will be coming to America to compete."

Megan, like everyone else, had heard of these games. They were held every year, with a dif-ferent country hosting them each time. She could remember watching some of the events on television.

What does this have to do with Camp Sunnyside, she wondered. Ms. Winkle answered her silent question.

"On Tuesday, the girls' gymnastics team from Baldavia will be arriving here at our camp. They will stay here to practice for a week, before going on to New York."

A murmur went through the room. "Baldavia," Trina said. "I wonder where that is?"

"I think it's a small country in Eastern Europe," Carolyn told them.

"Girls, I haven't finished!" Ms. Winkle's voice was rising. "Please, listen to me. This year is the first time Baldavia has sent a team to an international competition. I doubt that any of these girls has ever been to the United States before. And I'm certain they've never seen a summer camp. Coming here will be a strange new experience for them, and I want all of you to make them feel welcome."

The camp director became very serious. "This is more important than any of you may realize. You see, the old government of Baldavia didn't always get along with the government of our country. But they have a new government now, and the United States is trying to establish a good relationship. In our own way, we can play a part in helping the two countries become friends. You campers will probably be the first

Americans the Baldavian girls have ever met. I'm always telling you girls that when visitors come here, each of you represents Camp Sunnyside. With these visitors, you represent even more. Each and every one of you represents the United States of America!"

A shiver went up Megan's spine. She realized that the room had become utterly, totally silent.

"Whatever these gymnasts think about you, that's what they'll think about our country. So let's show this team a wonderful time. Let's make sure they leave here feeling good about America!"

By the time she finished, Ms. Winkle's face was red. This was the longest speech Megan could remember Ms. Winkle ever making. And it seemed to have had quite an effect on the campers. Gazing around, Megan saw widened eyes and awed expressions all over the room. But when she turned to her own cabin mates, all she saw on their faces was mild curiosity.

She tried to pump up some enthusiasm. "Wow, what a speech!"

"It was certainly long enough," Katie remarked.

"I don't know about you guys," Megan continued, "but I've got goose bumps!"

"Are you cold?" Trina asked.

Megan was getting more and more frustrated. "No, I'm not cold. I'm excited! Weren't you listening to what Ms. Winkle said?"

"I guess it could be interesting to watch championship gymnasts practice," Trina commented.

"Yeah, if you're into gymnastics," Sarah said. "I tried the vault once, and practically broke my legs."

Erin made a face. "Too bad we couldn't get the *boys'* gymnastics team."

Carolyn laughed. "If we had the boys' team here, Erin, you'd try to make every one of them fall madly in love with you. Why, you might start an international incident! Personally, I think we're better off with girls." She rose. "Excuse me, kids, I have to see Ms. Winkle about something."

Megan barely noticed her departure. Her mind was spinning. Why didn't the girls see the possibilities in this? Here was the opportunity she'd been waiting for to get them all out of the doldrums.

"Megan, what's up?" Sarah demanded to know.

"What do you mean?" Megan asked.

"You've got that funny little gleam in your

11

eye," Sarah replied. "And we all know what that means."

Katie nodded wisely. "She's off in fantasy land. Let me guess what you're daydreaming about." She paused thoughtfully. "Okay, how about this. You're working out on the balance beam in the gym. The Baldavian team walks in and sees you. They're so impressed with your talent that they make you an honorary citizen of Baldavia so you can play in the One World Games with them."

Sarah joined in. "And you score a perfect ten in every event. Baldavia wins the championship. Only then, a newspaper reporter discovers that you're actually an American. The world will think you were kidnapped by the team."

"Or they'll think you're a spy!" Erin said. "And you'll create a, a—what did Carolyn call it? An international incident!"

Trina was smiling, but she scolded them. "Quit teasing her, you guys."

Megan didn't mind the teasing. She had something more important on her mind. "Listen, what Ms. Winkle said was really serious. We have to give these girls a good impression of us. We don't want them telling everyone back in Baldavia that America's a terrible place."

"Don't worry, Megan," Trina said. "We'll be nice to them."

"But we have to be more than nice," Megan persisted. "We have to make them love us! Like Ms. Winkle said, the United States is just starting to be friendly with Baldavia. We want them to believe this is a great country."

"And just how are we supposed to do that?" Sarah asked.

Megan leaned forward. "Remember when we were in Italy, how strange and unfamiliar everything seemed?"

"Not for long," Erin said. "We had Enrico." She sighed deeply and rested her chin in her hand. The others exchanged meaningful looks. Enrico had been working at the hotel where the girls had stayed in Rome, and he'd been wonderful to them all. Of course, Erin had developed a major crush on him.

"Enrico was more than nice to us," Megan went on. "He made us see how wonderful Italy is. We need to do the same thing for the girls from Baldavia." She watched their expressions eagerly, hoping for some show of support.

Slowly, Katie nodded. "I think Megan's right. We want these girls to love this country, the way we loved Italy."

"Exactly!" Megan proclaimed, happy to have

13

Katie on her side. If she could get Katie to go along with her plans, the others would follow. "When the team goes back to Baldavia, we want them to tell everyone that America is fantastic!"

Finally, her enthusiasm began to catch on. "Megan, you're absolutely right," Sarah said. "We'll let them know Americans are the nicest people on earth."

"And that Camp Sunnyside is the best summer camp in the world," Trina put in.

Erin rolled her eyes. "That shouldn't be too hard. Like Ms. Winkle said, these girls have probably never *been* to a summer camp before."

Katie shot her a fierce look. "Come on, Erin. We've all got to be in on this together. Promise you'll go along with us."

"Yeah, yeah, sure."

Megan wasn't worried about Erin. Except for boys, clothes, and makeup, Erin never got excited about much. Besides, she was feeling too good to worry about anything. The other girls were talking now, and they looked more upbeat than they had in ages. She, Megan Lindsay, had put the spirit back into cabin six.

With a little help from Baldavia.

Chapter 2

During free period on Tuesday, the cabin six girls met in the arts and crafts cabin. They went to the table where they'd left the banner they'd made earlier. Megan grabbed one end, Katie grabbed the other, and they unrolled it. The other girls gathered round to examine it.

"Welcome Friends," Sarah read aloud. "It looks nice."

Some of the older girls from cabin nine wandered over to see the banner. Megan frowned as she noticed that one of them was Maura Kingsley, the nastiest girl at Sunnyside.

Maura raised her eyebrows as she read the banner. "What's that for?"

"It's to welcome the gymnastics team from Baldavia," Megan told her.

Maura made a face. "Personally, I'm not crazy about the idea of foreigners coming to

Sunnyside." She was addressing her remarks to the other thirteen year olds with her, but she spoke loud enough for everyone in the cabin to hear. "I mean, it would be okay if these girls were from England or France, someplace nice like that. But who wants visitors from some dumb little country that no one's ever even heard of?"

Her buddies nodded in agreement.

"And who knows what these girls could be like?" Maura continued. "We don't know anything about Baldavia. Maybe it's not a very civilized country. These girls might not even be clean."

Megan could see Katie was about to lose her temper. "Don't be stupid. They're championship gymnasts, for crying out loud!"

"That doesn't mean they're going to be clean," Maura snapped back.

Even mild-mannered Trina was getting annoyed. "This is a silly conversation."

"No kidding," Sarah said. "Look, Maura, if they're not clean, we'll let them use our showers, okay?"

Erin started giggling, but she stopped when Maura shot her a dirty look. Erin was still a little impressed by the older girls.

Katie edged toward Megan and whispered in

16

her ear. "We'd better not let Maura near the gymnasts. If they think *she* represents America, we might end up at war with Baldavia."

Megan grinned, and turned her attention back to the banner. Donna, the arts and crafts counselor, joined them. "That banner looks good."

"Do you think we should make it more personal?" Trina asked. "Like, Welcome to Our New Friends from Baldavia?"

Donna shook her head. "No, they might not know English very well. Keep it plain and simple, just as it is. They'll get the message."

Maura sniffed. "It seems to me that if people are going to visit this country, they should learn how to speak English."

Megan glanced at her uneasily. Maybe she should take Katie's warning seriously. With that attitude, Maura was fully capable of starting a war.

Carolyn came into the cabin. "The bus is due in just a few minutes, girls. Ready?"

Quickly, Megan and Katie rolled the banner up. As they headed for the door, they heard Maura laughing. Loudly, she proclaimed, "There they go, Sunnyside's own little welcoming committee. You guys better not be *too* nice to those gymnasts. They might not ever leave."

"Oh, I wouldn't worry about that," one of her friends called out. "One looks at the cabin six crowd, and they'll probably race back to Baldavia."

"Why do they act like that?" Sarah groaned as they walked toward Ms. Winkle's office.

"They're just teasing," Carolyn replied. "Ignore them."

"That's easy for us to do," Megan said worriedly. "I hope the girls from Baldavia can ignore them too."

Along the way, she looked at the cabins they passed. "Funny, I never noticed before how shabby some of those cabins look. I wish they could have been painted before our visitors arrived here."

Carolyn put a comforting hand on her shoulder. "It's okay, Megan. These girls aren't expecting paradise."

But that was exactly what Megan wanted them to see. She was relieved when they arrived at Ms. Winkle's cabin, where the bus carrying the gymnasts was supposed to stop. At least other campers didn't have the same attitude as cabin nine. There was a whole crowd gathered there. Ms. Winkle, a hand shading her eyes, peered down the road. Then she began waving.

"Here they come!" Megan said excitedly. She and Katie unfurled the banner and held it over their heads. As the bus passed, she could see several faces behind the windows. She wondered how the Sunnyside campers looked to the girls in the bus.

The bus came to a halt, and Ms. Winkle hurried over to the door. When it opened, the first person to come off was a woman. She was followed by eight girls. Ms. Winkle signaled a counselor, who blew into a pitch pipe. All of the campers burst into the official Camp Sunnyside song. Megan sang out with feeling, loudly and lustily.

I'm a Sunnyside girl, with a Sunnyside smile,
And I spend my summers in Sunnyside style,
I have sunny, sunny times with my Sunnyside
*   friends,*
And I know I'll be sad when the summer ends,
But I'll always remember, with joy and pride,
My sunny, sunny days at Sunnyside!

Megan looked for a reaction from the Baldavian girls. They were staring at the campers with dazed expressions.

"They certainly look clean to me," Katie whispered to Megan.

19

Megan nodded. If the gymnasts had been wearing Sunnyside tee shirts, like the campers, they'd have looked no different from the campers. But she didn't get much of a chance to look them over. The woman hurried them into Ms. Winkle's office. Then she spoke with Ms. Winkle, and Ms. Winkle blew her whistle. "Girls, this is Miss, uh . . . ," she stumbled over the unusual name, which sounded something like Brizwee. "She is the Baldavian gymnastics coach, and she would like to speak with you."

The woman stepped forward, and Megan got a good look at her. Her gray hair was pulled back tightly, and her face was stern. "Girls, the Baldavian team thanks you for your warm welcome," she said, with a pretty accent. "The gymnasts have had a very long journey, and they will be going directly to their cabin. They look forward to spending the week at your camp, and will not interfere with your routine." She disappeared inside the cabin with Ms. Winkle.

"Hey, can we put this banner down now?" Katie asked. "My arm's hurting."

Megan's shoulders drooped as she dropped the banner. "Is that it? Aren't we even going to meet them?"

"They're probably tired," Sarah said.

"I'm sure we'll get a chance later, at dinner," Carolyn assured them. Megan nodded. Still, after all the anticipation, it was kind of a letdown.

She was still feeling let down two days later. "I can't believe this," she complained at lunch. "We haven't even met any of them yet!"

"And it doesn't look like we're going to," Trina said. She took a furtive peek at the table where the Baldavian team was eating, way at the end of the dining hall. "For every meal, they've been sitting by themselves. I guess they don't want to mingle with us."

"This is the only place where we ever see them," Katie noted. "Do they practice all day?"

Megan refused to believe that. "Nobody can practice gymnastics all day."

"I heard they were at the pool yesterday," Erin told them. "When none of the cabins were there."

"I guess they just want to stick together," Sarah said. "It certainly doesn't look like they want to hang out with any campers."

Carolyn smiled. "Or maybe they're waiting for some campers to approach them first."

Erin took a look at the Baldavians and shuddered. "I wouldn't want to go over there right now and approach them. That coach looks *mean.*"

"All coaches look mean," Megan told her. "That's part of their job."

They all watched as the team rose from their seats, formed a line, and returned their trays. Then they filed out of the dining hall.

"They don't look like they're having much fun," Megan said sadly. "None of them is smiling."

"I've got an idea," Katie said. "If we can skip archery, we could go to the gym and watch them practice. Then maybe we could strike up conversations."

Eager eyes turned to Carolyn for permission. None of the girls much liked archery.

Carolyn considered the request. "I don't think all of you should go at the same time. That might intimidate them. Maybe just two of you could watch them."

Sarah spoke up. "Then it should be Megan and Katie. Megan, because it was her idea to get to know these girls. And Katie because she's the most friendly."

Megan grinned at her. She thought Sarah was just as friendly as Katie, but it was true that Katie was the most outgoing.

As soon as lunch was over, Megan and Katie ran to the gym. From the doorway, they could see the team practicing. The Baldavian coach was calling out directions in a language they couldn't understand. One by one, each of the team members jumped over the vault. No one noticed as Katie and Megan edged along the wall and took seats on the bleachers. They sat there quietly and watched the practice.

"Wow!" Megan exclaimed. "They're really good!"

"No kidding!" Katie agreed.

The team had split up, and girls were working on different events. One girl seemed to fly as she swung between the parallel bars. Another one practically skipped across the balance beam. A third girl, alone on a mat, was executing a freestyle program that looked like a combination of ballet and acrobatics.

But there was one girl who really stood out. She looked like she was about their age, although she was shorter and had powerful muscles. Her body twisted and bent in a way that Megan wouldn't have thought was possible, as if she were made out of rubber or something. She walked the balance beam on her hands, and her legs weren't even shaking. On the parallel bars, she seemed to hang suspended in the air before doing a double flip.

Megan thought she was amazing. But the coach never seemed pleased with the girl's performance—or anyone else's, for that matter. She made the girls repeat their moves over and over. Megan wondered how they felt about this. She remembered a particularly brutal tennis coach she'd had once, during a tournament. He'd been so tough on her that he made her want to quit tennis forever. Even though Megan couldn't understand what the gymnastics coach was saying, she suspected her style was the same as that of her former tennis coach. She couldn't help feeling a little sorry for the team.

Finally, the coach blew her whistle, and the girls stopped. They picked up towels and threw them around their necks. "Here's our chance," Katie said. She and Megan scrambled off the bleachers and approached the group. A few glanced curiously at them, and then averted their eyes.

Megan grinned, and she was about to say hi when the coach blew her whistle again. Immediately, the team formed a line and began to walk out.

Megan and Katie stared after them. "This is

weird," Katie growled. "Don't they want to meet us?"

Megan shivered. "It's creepy. Hey, maybe it's the coach. Maybe *she* doesn't want them to meet us."

"That's silly," Katie replied. "Why would the coach care if they talk to us?"

Megan dug into her imagination, a bottomless pit of fantasies. "Remember what Ms. Winkle said, about how our countries were just beginning to become friendly? Well, maybe this coach doesn't want our countries to be friends." She clutched Katie's arm. "Maybe they're not even a gymnastics team. Maybe they're a bunch of spies!"

"Give me a break," Katie groaned. "Megan, you just saw them. Spies can't swing on parallel bars like that!"

"How do you know? When did you ever meet a spy?"

"Shh," Katie hissed. "Here comes one of them."

The small, muscular girl who had performed so incredibly was walking back into the gym. When she passed Megan and Katie, she ducked her head. But Megan could have sworn she was giving them the once-over with a sidelong look. And there was the hint of a smile on her face.

25

The girl was searching the gym looking for something. Megan stepped forward. "Hi!"

The girl stepped back, her eyes wide, and didn't speak. Megan tried again. "Do you speak English?"

"Yes," the girl said softly.

"Can we help you?" Katie asked. "Are you looking for something?"

"Yes. My . . ." she hesitated. "What do you call it? Oh yes, my towel."

The girls looked around. Megan got up on a bleacher and peered between the tiers. "Here it is. It fell inside." She reached down and pulled it up.

"Thank you," the girl said, taking the towel. She turned to leave.

"Wait!" Megan cried out. The girl stopped and looked back.

"Uh, what's your name?" Megan asked.

She thought the girl seemed strangely nervous when she answered. "Karina."

"That's a pretty name. I'm Megan, and this is Katie. We're campers."

"Nice to meet you," Katie said.

Karina gave them a slight smile. "How do you do?" Then she started toward the door.

"Wait!" Megan called again. Boldly, she faced Karina. "Why don't you want to talk to us?"

Karina's expression was bewildered. "What do you mean?"

Megan fumbled with her words. "Well, you guys haven't been too friendly. I mean, your team has been here two days, and we haven't talked at all."

"Yeah," Katie said. "And we were looking forward to meeting you guys."

"Guys?" Karina's brow furrowed. "Excuse me, please. My English is not perfect. But I believe we are what you call in English girls. Not guys."

Megan grinned. "Yeah, you're right. But it's slang, you know? We use the word *guys* for just about anyone."

Karina still looked confused, but she smiled. "Very interesting. I know so little about your language. Or your country."

"Would you like to know more?" Megan asked eagerly.

Suddenly, that nervous look appeared on her face again. "Um, I must go now." She started walking, but Katie and Megan ran after her.

Katie reached her first. And in her typically no-nonsense way, she got right to the point. "Karina, why are you scared of us?"

Karina drew herself up stiffly. "Scared? I am not scared of you."

27

Katie put her hands on her hips. "Oh yeah? Then maybe you're just a snob."

"Snob?" Karina repeated the word carefully. "I do not know what this word means."

Megan tried not to let her own frustration show. "It means someone who thinks she's better than anyone else."

Katie nodded. "Right. I guess just because you guys are big-shot gymnasts, you think you're too good to talk to wimpy, ordinary campers."

Megan suspected that Karina wouldn't know what big-shot or wimpy meant, but Karina got the tone behind the words. She gasped.

"Oh no! This is not true! We are not . . . what was the word you used? Snobs. No, no, we do not think we are better than anybody." An actual full smile appeared. "Except, perhaps, we hope we are better in gymnastics than the other teams we will be facing."

"Then why won't you talk to us?" Megan asked. "Why don't you want to get to know us?"

Karina sighed. "We have strict orders from our coach. We are not to bother you campers. Our coach says we must not interfere with your routine or disturb your activities."

Megan's mouth fell open. "Are you kidding? We *love* being disturbed!"

"That's why we were excited about your coming to Sunnyside," Katie added. "Things were getting boring around here."

Now it was Karina's turn to show disbelief. "Boring? Here? How is that possible?"

"It's definitely possible," Katie insisted. "Things are pretty much the same here every day."

"I do not understand," Karina said. "Of course, I have never seen a place such as this before. We do not have summer camps in Baldavia."

"Then you should be having a real summer camp experience," Megan declared. "Why don't you and your team hang out with us tomorrow?"

Karina carefully repeated, "Hang out?"

"You know, *be* with us," Megan said. "Do you have to practice all day?"

"No," Karina said. "We have three one-hour sessions each day. Actually, tomorrow we have a holiday from practice."

"Super!" Katie exclaimed. "Then bring your teammates, and meet us tomorrow morning at cabin six."

"You guys can spend the whole day with us," Megan told her. "With me and Katie and the rest of our cabin mates. You can see what a summer camp is really like. We can learn about Baldavia, you can learn about America. How about it?"

There was a sparkle in Karina's eyes. "Oh, that would be a very interesting experience. I will speak with my teammates. Of course, we shall have to get permission from our coach. Have you received permission to issue this kind invitation to us?"

"Don't worry about that," Katie assured her. "We do pretty much anything we want."

There was doubt in Karina's eyes. But she smiled. "Then perhaps we shall meet tomorrow." She headed toward the door.

"Cabin six," Megan called after her.

Karina turned, nodded, and waved.

"This is great," Katie said happily. "It's just like Carolyn said. They were waiting for us to make the first move."

Megan agreed. "I feel like we've been on a peace mission." She cocked her head thoughtfully. "You know, Katie, I think the government should send people like us to countries where people don't get along. Like the Middle East, or Ireland . . . and we could teach people how to be friends with each other."

Katie grinned. "Don't get carried away, Megan. I don't think we're exactly qualified yet to make world peace. Let's just see how we get along with the gymnasts from Baldavia."

Chapter 3

The next morning, as the cabin six girls got ready for breakfast, Megan gave her cabin mates some last-minute instructions. "Now, remember, no complaining today. And no acting bored, or anything like that."

"Right," Katie said. "These girls have been cooped up for days. They need some fun. And some freedom!" She made a face. "The way that coach makes them march in single file— they look like they're in the army, or something!"

"Why have they been acting so snobby?" Sarah asked.

"Karina said they're not snobs," Megan told her. "When we talked to her, she acted like they were . . . scared."

Erin's expression was incredulous. "Scared? Of us?"

Katie nodded. "Strange, huh? But she said their coach told them not to disturb us. Personally, I still think she's a little scared."

Erin considered that. "Maybe we just seem terribly sophisticated to them."

Sarah snorted. "Megan and Katie? Sophisticated?"

Katie tossed a pillow at her, but Trina caught it in midair. "Well, they *are* from another country," she noted as she returned the pillow to Katie's bed. "They don't know how friendly we can be."

"We can show them today," Megan stated with confidence. "We'll make sure they see how super American people are, and how they've got nothing to be afraid of."

Erin spoke carefully. "Do they seem very . . . foreign?"

Megan laughed. "They're perfectly clean, Erin, if that's what you mean." She looked out the window. There was no sign yet of the Baldavians. "Just be sure to make everything about Sunnyside sound absolutely wonderful. And everything in America. Even if we have to exaggerate a little."

Katie agreed. "We want them to leave here with great impressions."

Carolyn came out of her room. "It's time for breakfast."

"But we have to wait for the team!" Megan protested.

"Maybe they're planning to meet us in the dining hall," Trina suggested.

"No," Megan replied, "I clearly told Karina, cabin six. Didn't I, Katie?"

"Yeah. But she said they had to get permission. Maybe they didn't get it."

"That coach must be a real witch," Erin commented.

Megan bit her lip. "Carolyn, do you think maybe the coach hates Americans? She could be keeping them against their will!"

"Megan, you're letting your imagination run away with you," Carolyn scolded. "Now, let's go. We can't wait any longer."

Megan lingered as the group left. Then, dragging her feet, she followed.

"Hello! Wait, please!"

Megan's disappointment evaporated. "Karina! You're here! Come meet my cabin mates." Karina approached shyly as Megan began the introductions.

"This is Erin, this is Sarah, and that's Trina. This is our counselor, Carolyn. Everyone, meet Karina."

34

With a serious expression, Karina shook hands, and kept repeating, "I am pleased to meet you." When she reached Carolyn, she looked like she was about to curtsey. "I thank you for granting permission to have me join you today."

Carolyn laughed. "No one asked *my* permission! But you're very welcome, Karina."

"Let's go, or there won't be any food left," Sarah urged. The girls hurried toward the dining hall.

"Where are your teammates?" Katie asked Karina.

"Our coach has arranged an outing. To the town nearby."

"Pine Ridge?" Megan frowned. "That's not too thrilling. Did you tell them they were all invited to join us?"

"Yes. I asked if they would like to . . . how did you say it? Hang out. But they preferred to stay together, alone."

"Weird," Katie muttered under her breath.

Erin didn't bother to hide her reaction. "If I was with the same girls all day, I'd be dying to meet some new people."

"You *are* with the same girls all day," Sarah reminded her.

"Right! And I'm dying to meet some new people!"

Katie poked Erin with her elbow. "What was that for?" Erin yelped. She rolled her eyes as she remembered Megan's instructions. "Of course, I absolutely *love* my cabin mates," she added.

In the dining hall, the girls got their trays and brought them to their table. Carolyn followed them, but she didn't sit down. "You'll have to excuse me. I've got a meeting with some counselors. I hope you have a nice day, Karina."

Karina was examining her tray. "What is this?"

"Blueberry pancakes," Trina told her.

"That's how we know it's Friday," Sarah added. "Every Friday, it's blueberry pancakes for breakfast."

"Try some syrup with them," Megan said.

Karina took a small, tentative bite. Her eyes grew the size of saucers. "This is delicious! Never in my life have I tasted something like this!"

Sarah whispered in Megan's ears. "She's going a little overboard with the compliments, isn't she?"

Megan was too busy chewing to answer. The

36

pancakes *were* good. Actually, they tasted even better than usual.

"It's too bad your teammates couldn't be with us today," Trina said.

"Yeah," Erin said, "Don't they *want* to meet us?"

Karina stopped eating. She glanced over her shoulder, as if she feared someone would be listening.

"You can tell us," Megan said. "Why didn't they want to hang out with us?"

Karina appeared to be choosing her words very carefully. "Well, they have heard some stories about Americans."

Erin nodded wisely. "Oh, I get it. They think we're going to be very elegant and sophisticated, and they'll feel dumb around us."

"No, that is not it," Karina said. "Of course, I am sure the rumors are not true. But we hear that Americans are rude, and greedy, and violent. And they are always fighting."

Katie laughed. "I think the Baldavians have seen too many Arnold Schwarzenegger movies."

Karina's eyes lit up. "Yes! We see those movies in Baldavia. Also, the movies about Freddy Kruger."

"Good grief!" Megan exclaimed. "Please, don't think those movies are true! We're not like

37

that at all! At least, not here at Sunnyside. Nobody gets violent."

"I'd never get into a fight with anyone," Erin declared.

"Unless someone stole your cosmetic case," Sarah countered.

Karina's face broke into a real smile. And she actually giggled. "Yes, I can see you are not like the people we see in movies."

"I'll bet it's nice being away from your teammates," Erin said.

Karina stopped laughing. "Why do you say that?"

Erin shrugged. "Well, anyone would get bored with the same people, doing the same thing, everyday."

"Yeah," Sarah agreed. "We even get bored here." After a sharp look from Megan, she amended that. "But not very often. Hardly ever, actually."

Megan gazed at Karina's pale face in concern. "What's wrong? Don't you like your teammates?"

Again, Karina looked around furtively. "I think, perhaps, some of them do not like me." Then she put a hand over her mouth, as if she regretted saying that.

But Megan could tell she wanted to talk about it. "Why wouldn't your teammates like you?"

"I am younger than they are," Karina said. "And . . . ," she hesitated.

Katie guessed. "You're a better gymnast than they are."

"That's right, we saw you," Megan said.

Karina blushed. Trina reached across the table and patted her arm. "They're probably just jealous."

Karina smiled slightly, but for the third time she looked over her shoulder.

"Why are you worried that someone might hear you?" Sarah asked.

"It is important that we are loyal to each other," Karina explained. "We have to perform as a united team."

Megan understood that. Cabin six had been through competitions every summer at camp, and no matter how much they disagreed with each other, they had to stick together.

Karina continued. "The coach would be very angry if I said anything about the others."

Recalling her earlier suspicions, Megan asked, "Are you afraid of her?"

Karina gazed down at her plate. "She is very . . . strict."

Carolyn returned. "Time to get back to the cabin for inspection."

"What is inspection?" Karina asked Megan as they walked out.

"No big deal," Megan told her. "We just have to straighten up the cabin."

Back in the cabin, the girls hurriedly made their beds, and stuffed clothes into drawers. As usual, Erin moaned and groaned over the little chores. "Back home, I never make my bed," she told Karina.

Karina was surprised. "You don't?"

"Of course not. We have a maid."

Megan considered telling Karina that not everyone in America had servants, but Karina looked so impressed she decided not to. The little gymnast wandered around the cabin, helping to smooth sheets and straighten bedspreads. When she got to Megan's bed, she exclaimed, "Megan, there is a lump on your bed!"

Carolyn came in. She walked the length of the room, glancing from right to left. "Okay, you can go to the pool."

"She didn't see the lump on your bed!" Karina whispered.

"It wouldn't matter if she did," Megan told her. "Carolyn's not very strict."

"You are fortunate," Karina sighed.

Megan loaned Karina a bathing suit, and the girls changed. Then they headed to the pool.

"Who is that man?" Karina asked, peering down the side of the pool.

"That's Darrell, the swimming coach," Trina told her.

Automatically, all the cabin six girls put their hands over their hearts and swooned, like they always did when Darrell's name was mentioned.

"Does he tell you what to do?" Karina asked.

"Sometimes," Trina replied. "When we have classes."

"But mostly we just do whatever we want," Katie said. "Like today. It's free swim day." She raced ahead and jumped into the water. The others followed, except for Erin, who sat on the edge and dangled her feet in the water.

Karina stood in the water, taking in the scene. All around her, campers were yelling and screeching, splashing and dunking each other.

"Erin, come on in!" Katie yelled.

Erin shrank back from the splashing. "I don't want to get my hair wet."

"Oh," Katie said. "Okay." She turned away from Erin. Then, suddenly, she whirled around, and with her entire arm sent a huge spray of water directly at her.

"Katie!" Erin shrieked. "You creep!"

"Don't get mad," Megan hissed at her. "Come on, show Karina how much fun we have!"

Erin touched her hair. It was already wet. With a sigh, and a forced smile, she lowered herself into the water.

Karina still just stood there, gaping. But it didn't take long for her to get into the spirit of the scene. Katie got hold of a frisbee, and the girls began tossing it back and forth. It was clear that Karina had never played with a frisbee before, but she caught on right away.

"I'll get it! I'll get it!" Karina called as the disk came flying her way. Backing up, she collided with a pair of legs dangling down the side. Unfortunately, those legs belonged to Maura Kingsley.

"Watch it!" Maura yelled in outrage.

Karina didn't catch her tone. "Come on in," she cried out in a good imitation of Katie.

Maura glared at her. "I don't want to get my hair wet."

Karina turned away. Then she whirled around, smiling, and sent a jet of water directly into Maura's face.

Megan watched in horror as Maura's face

went red with fury. "How dare you!" Maura's eyes narrowed. "Aren't you one of those *gymnasts?*" She made the word *gymnasts* sound like she meant disgusting slime.

Karina couldn't miss the tone this time. She edged backwards. "Yes, I am from Baldavia."

Maura spoke to no one in particular. "Foreigners! They have no manners at all!" She rose and marched away.

Karina looked like she was about to burst into tears. Megan and Katie hastened to her side.

"Don't mind her," Katie said.

"Yeah, she's not a typical American," Megan assured her. "And she's definitely not a typical Sunnyside girl."

"But I have offended her," Karina moaned. "Now she may tell my coach."

"She won't tell her," Katie said. "She just likes to make a lot of noise."

"No one pays any attention to her," Megan declared.

Still, Karina seemed distressed. And Megan was angry. She pulled Katie aside.

"I *hate* that Maura Kingsley," she sputtered. "She could ruin everything."

"We'll just have to keep Karina away from her," Katie said.

43

"And we have to make up for any bad impression she gave of America," Megan added. There was no way she was going to let Maura ruin their plans.

Chapter 4

From the pool, the girls went back to the cabin to change. "Karina, I've got an extra Camp Sunnyside tee shirt you can wear," Megan offered.

Karina handled the tee shirt as if it were a gown. "But what if I make it dirty?"

Megan shrugged. "We'll send it to the laundry."

Karina slipped it on. "It is very nice."

"Now you look like one of us," Katie proclaimed. "A real Sunnyside girl!"

Karina smiled with pleasure. She seemed to be recovering from her run-in with Maura. "Where do we go now?"

"Archery," Trina told her.

"It's boring," Sarah started to say, and then quickly added, "But we still have fun."

They all trooped over to the archery range.

Karina had never used bows and arrows before, and the archery counselor demonstrated the technique.

Karina strung her bow and took an arrow. She stood before a target and made her first attempt.

"Bull's-eye!" Trina cried out. "That's amazing! I've been doing this for years, and I've never hit the center!"

"You are right," Karina cried in glee. "This *is* fun! I like archery!"

And for once, Megan had to agree. Seeing archery through Karina's eyes made it a whole different sport. Megan found herself pretending to be Robin Hood, making a real effort to aim properly, and getting excited when she actually hit the target.

The others were getting into it too. Sarah started keeping score, and Katie got into a real competitive spirit. They began yelling and cheering, and soon the counselor was staring at them in disbelief. Megan couldn't blame her. None of them had ever shown any enthusiasm for archery before.

"It's so beautiful here," Karina said as they left the archery range. "Look at those flowers! Do they grow wild? What is their name?"

Sarah took a close look. "They're tiger lilies.

Gee, I've never noticed them before. They *are* pretty."

"And all these trees!" Karina paused to peer over a ridge. "That lake . . . I saw it when we arrived on the bus. Are you allowed to go to the lake?"

"Of course we are," Erin said. "The lake belongs to Camp Sunnyside."

"We take canoes out on the lake sometimes," Trina told her.

"Canoes!" Karina exclaimed. "How glorious!"

Glorious wasn't a word Megan had ever associated with canoes before. But then she thought about some of their canoe races. She recalled the rhythm of paddling, the warm breeze, the sensation of bobbing on the calm water. Yes, maybe glorious *was* a good word for it.

Karina oohed and ahhed over all the stuff in the arts and crafts cabin. And when they went to lunch, she went crazy over the lasagna.

"Have you been having a good time today, Karina?" Carolyn asked her.

"I have never had such a good time," Karina replied. "You are all so kind to organize this special day for me."

"It's nothing special," Megan said casually. "Just a typical Sunnyside day."

Karina cocked her head and looked puzzled. "But when do you work? Or study?"

"This is summer camp," Katie said. "It's just good times, that's it."

"And the food at Sunnyside, it is always this delicious?" Karina asked.

"Sure," Megan responded. "It's just good ol' American cooking."

Trina didn't do a very good job of hiding her smile, and Megan knew why. After a trip to Italy, she should know better than to call lasagna good ol' American food!

"Sunnyside food *is* pretty terrific," Sarah stated. "I hope we have macaroni and cheese before you leave. That's the best."

"What kind of food do you eat in Baldavia?" Trina asked in interest.

Karina waved a hand vaguely. "Oh, meat, vegetables, fruit, like that . . . but it is not as good as this. Is all American food this good?"

"No one better tell her about brussels sprouts," Sarah whispered to Megan.

"American food's great," Megan said.

"It is this good at your schools, too?"

Megan could see Katie practically choking. And all the girls were exchanging looks. Megan figured all school lunches were pretty much the same—basically disgusting. But it wouldn't do to let Karina hear that. "Oh, sure, the food at school is great too."

"Absolutely delicious," Sarah said.

"Fantastic," Katie echoed. But when Karina wasn't looking, she made a gagging expression.

Carolyn was gazing at them all with a curious expression. "My goodness, school lunches must have changed radically since my school days."

Katie finished eating first. "Hurry up, you guys. I want to get to the stables before someone else takes Starfire."

"What is Starfire?" Karina asked.

"Only the very best horse in the Sunnyside stables," Katie replied.

"You have horses here?" Karina said in wonderment. "For riding?"

"Of course," Megan stated, with a dramatic wave of her hand. "Sunnyside has everything!"

"Come on, let's go!" Katie said urgently. The girls began to rise.

"Don't you have to ask permission?" Karina asked Megan in an undertone.

"Ask permission from who?"

"From the counselor, Carolyn."

Katie overheard this. "Heck no. At Sunnyside, we do what we want, when we want to do it."

That was definitely an exaggeration, Megan

thought. If not an out-and-out lie. There were rules at Sunnyside, and Carolyn had been known to put her foot down. But she didn't contradict Katie. After all, they wanted Karina to feel that at Sunnyside, she didn't have to worry about rules or restrictions. They wanted Karina to feel like she was in paradise. And in paradise, no one should have to ask for permission to do anything.

They had a great time riding that afternoon. The sun was shining, and the horses were in high spirits. Katie even let Karina have a ride on Starfire.

Afterwards, as they led the horses back to the stable, Karina said, "You must feel terrible at the end of the summer, when you leave this place."

"But the rest of America is pretty super too," Megan told her.

"And we see each other during the school year," Katie said. "Last October, we all got together at Megan's. At Christmas, we all went skiing. And during the spring break, we all took a trip to Italy."

"Don't forget the wedding," Sarah reminded her.

"Right!" Katie explained to Karina. "Sarah's

father married Trina's mother. We all went to the wedding."

"We have great times all year long, not just in the summer," Megan said.

"But what about school?" Karina asked.

"We get lots of holidays from school in America," Erin said.

Katie grinned. "In fact, we hardly go at all!"

"And when we do go," Megan added, "we don't have to work very hard."

"Megan!" Trina's face was clearly disapproving. Luckily, Karina didn't see that.

"You are so lucky," Karina sighed. "But at your homes—surely, you must work there. You have chores, or perhaps a young brother or sister to care for."

No kidding, Megan thought, thinking about her own baby brother and the list of chores that had a permanent place on the refrigerator. She wasn't surprised to hear Erin say, "I don't do any chores." But she *was* startled to hear Katie announce, "In America, kids don't do many chores."

Well, she *had* told everyone to exaggerate if necessary. But Trina was really frowning now. She pulled Megan aside. "Megan, we shouldn't be telling her *lies.*" Megan smiled weakly.

"America is nothing like I expected it to be," Karina said dreamily.

"Because we don't carry guns?" Sarah asked jokingly.

"It is not just that," Karina said. "I thought that in America, people worked all the time, even young people. I thought they studied a great deal, too. I did not know that you have such an easy life!"

Megan beamed. "We're glad you like it here. Hey, guys, let's get some ice cream."

As they all ran to the ice cream stand, Karina looked like she was floating on a cloud. "Ice cream! I am hardly ever given permission to have ice cream. My coach does not allow us to eat anything except fruits between meals, and she does not approve of having many treats."

"What your coach doesn't know won't hurt her," Erin said gaily.

"We eat ice cream whenever we want," Sarah said. She patted her stomach. "It's too bad that I want it all the time."

Karina took a long time selecting her flavor. "Back in Baldavia, we only have vanilla," she told the others. She finally chose mint chocolate chip, and when she tasted it, she raised her eyes in ecstasy. "Ice cream! It is so . . . so wonderful!"

They ambled back toward the cabin. "It is almost time for me to return," Karina said. "I wish I did not have to leave you all. You have been so friendly."

"Why don't you spend the day with us tomorrow too?" Katie asked.

"I wish I could," Karina said. "But we have to work. Perhaps, I can receive permission to spend the time between practices with you."

"That would be great," Sarah said.

Karina paused, and her eyes swept over the group. When she spoke, her voice was wistful. "Do you campers always have this much fun?"

Megan replied firmly. "Always."

Chapter 5

The next day, the weather started off nice, but by mid-afternoon dark clouds began to appear. Sometimes it seemed to Megan that whenever the skies over Sunnyside threatened a summer drizzle, it was during free period.

At least no one in cabin six was acting bored this time. Karina was with them, so they all wore cheerful smiles and acted as if the crummy weather didn't bother them a bit. Karina sat on Erin's bed, looking and listening with enthusiastic interest as Erin went through her photo album.

"Here I am with my parents," Erin was saying. "And that's my best friend."

Megan had seen the album before, and so had all the other cabin six girls. They'd heard Erin's descriptions of every picture, and they'd endured Erin's bragging about her fancy house, her country club, her boyfriends and parties and dances. Usually, whenever Erin pulled out the humongous photo album, Sarah would shriek "close it," and Megan would make a big show of covering her ears. Katie, in particular, liked to tease Erin, and say that Erin should have her own television show—"Lifestyles of the Rich and Goofy."

But today, with Karina there, they didn't want to tease Erin or act like they'd heard these stories a million times. They had to fake something like serious fascination. It wasn't easy. Katie's smile was getting thinner and thinner. Sarah looked like she was ready to scream. Even Trina had a crease of pain running across her forehead.

"This is my ex-boyfriend, Alan," Erin said. "We broke up, but he keeps trying to get me to come back to him."

"He is very handsome," Karina said. "Are you permitted to date? In Baldavia, most girls are not allowed to date until they are fourteen or fifteen."

That was the age Megan's parents had told her *she* could date—if she even wanted to by then. But Erin laughed merrily. "Oh, here in America, kids grow up faster. Why, I think we have more freedom than just about any other place in the world. Anyway, here I am with Alan, in the back of his house."

Karina peered closely. "Is that a swimming pool?"

"Yes, it's in his back yard."

Karina's mouth fell open. "Americans have their own private swimming pools?"

"Not most Americans," Trina started to say, but Erin was saying, "Lots of my friends have swimming pools. Some have tennis courts, too." She turned a page. "Here I am, at a sleep-over party. My friends and I are watching videos."

"What is that?" Karina asked, pointing to something in the photograph.

"A wide-screen television. It's almost as big as a movie screen. Don't you have TVs in Baldavia?"

"Yes, but not like that."

Trina had to set the record straight. "Not that many people have wide-screen televisions, Karina. Why, I've never even seen one."

"How many televisions do you have in your home?" Karina asked her.

Trina thought. "Well, there's the one my mother and I had when we lived in the apartment . . ."

Sarah continued. "And we had two. So now there are three TVs in the house."

"Three televisions," Karina murmured. "We only have one. And it's small."

Erin went on. "Here's a picture of me, leaving for Italy. That's our car."

Megan remembered the first time the girls had come to Sunnyside, and their reaction when Erin arrived in a long limousine. Their eyes had popped out of their heads. Karina's reaction was no different. The gymnast shook her head in amazement. "Everything in America is so big! The buildings, the cars, the televisions . . . even the trees!"

"It's a big country," Erin said. "Really, the greatest country on earth! We're very lucky to be Americans."

As she talked, Megan stifled a yawn. Impressing a person could be exhausting, and they'd been doing that for two days now. Her thoughts went back to that morning. Karina had come in with her team, and the Baldavians had taken seats at their usual table. Megan noticed Karina looking at the cabin six table with longing. After a brief consultation with Carolyn, Megan gathered her nerve and went over there.

She tried not to look directly into the coach's steely eyes as she spoke to her. "We were wondering, my friends and me, uh, I, if Karina could come and sit with us?"

The coach didn't seem particularly thrilled with the notion. But she spoke to Karina in Baldavian, and Karina responded. The coach nodded, and Karina rose.

With Carolyn at the table, the girls couldn't exaggerate too much. But then Karina got permission from her coach to join them after her morning gymnastics session, and the girls spent the morning regaling her with grand stories.

Whatever they were doing, it was working. Karina seemed to love being with them. Everything they told her, about Sunnyside, America, their lives, impressed her. Of course, who wouldn't be impressed, Megan thought, the way they were blowing everything out of proportion!

Karina was very reluctant to leave them after lunch for her practice, and she returned to meet them immediately after. By now, Karina seemed to be completely convinced that all Americans were happy, fun-loving people who always got along with each other and spent their time eating great food, shopping, lolling on beaches, and traveling the world. And if she was assuming Erin's life was typical, she had to believe all Americans rode in limousines, swam in backyard pools, wore fancy clothes and generally lived in luxury. "This is my home," Erin was now saying.

"It is a palace!" Karina exclaimed. "Tell me, is everyone in America so rich?"

An image flashed before Megan's eyes—her own small home, with the shutters that were desperately in need of a coat of paint. It was a good thing Erin didn't have a picture of *that.*

Trina was squirming, and she looked distinctly uncomfortable. Sarah, too, seemed uneasy. "Uh, it's a funny thing. My grandfather used to tell my sister and me stories about when he first came to America, from Poland. He'd been very poor, and he expected the streets in America to be paved in gold."

"Were they?" Karina asked.

"Of course not!" Sarah said. "Those were just silly stories he'd heard back in Poland. In fact, when he got here, he had to live in one room, in an old, run-down building."

Megan caught puzzlement on Karina's face, so she quickly asked, "He didn't stay poor long, did he, Sarah?"

"Well, no. He started selling housewares from a pushcart. And he ended up owning a big store. He always told us that in America, anything is possible."

Karina smiled dreamily. "Ah, yes. That is what I am believing."

"Karina, we don't know anything about Baldavia," Trina said. "Tell us about your country."

That request was not received with great enthusiasm. "There is little to tell," Karina replied. "It is a very small country, not very interesting."

"Not to you, maybe," Trina said, "but to us it would be interesting. What's your life like there?"

Karina sighed, and then she began to tell them. "I live in a small house, with my mother and my father and my older sister."

Sarah, who also had an older sister, perked up at that. "Are you friends with your sister?"

Karina made a face. "She is very beautiful, and she acts very grand, and she always tells me what to do."

Sarah nodded wisely. "Bossy, huh?" Megan knew what was going through her head. Sarah's older sister was a counselor for a while at Sunnyside, and she was constantly ordering Sarah around.

"My sister and I are very different," Karina said. "She is neat, and I am a little messy. She likes quiet, and she becomes annoyed if I play the radio. Living together, sharing a room, it is very difficult. Sometimes she is impossible to live with. I am sure you do not have problems

60

like that." Sarah and Trina exchanged looks. As stepsisters, they were very different too, and Megan had heard tales from both of them about the problems they'd had getting along at home when their parents first got married.

"What about your parents?" Sarah asked. "Do they take sides with you or your sister?"

Karina scowled. "I believe they always agree with my sister. I get very angry. They do not try to understand my problems at all."

"Why don't you tell us about a typical day in your life," Trina urged.

"It is very boring," Karina said. "I wake up. I eat breakfast. I go to school. The school, it is not as you describe your school. We work very hard, and the teacher is very strict. After school, there is gymnastics. I go home, and I do homework. I am allowed to watch television for one hour, but my sister and I argue about which television program to watch."

"That's right, you said you only have one TV," Erin interrupted. "That's a pain. I have my very own, right in my bedroom."

"I am envious," Karina said. "My sister and I, we argue so much, my father makes the decision. And he always takes the side of my sister."

"I know what that's like," Katie muttered.

Megan knew she was thinking about her twin brothers. Katie always complained that her parents took their side.

"And then there are my chores," Karina continued. "I have to make my bed, and clean my room, and help wash the dishes every evening after our meal. Then there are special chores on the weekend, like dusting, or folding the sheets after my mother does the laundry." Except for Erin, Megan figured every girl in the room had similar chores at home. But no one mentioned them.

"That is my typical boring day," Karina finished. "It is very different from yours."

Actually, Megan was thinking that if you substituted tennis for gymnastics, her life wasn't that much different from Karina's.

"Don't you get together with friends?" Trina asked.

"There is very little time for that," Karina said. "Especially in this last year. I was very busy practicing, preparing for the One World Games."

"Your parents must be awfully proud of you," Katie said, "being on your country's gymnastics team."

Karina's face darkened. "They *say* they are proud. But I do not think they appreciate my work. What do American girls do with their friends?"

"Oh, we have lots of parties," Erin said. "And we hang out in the shopping mall . . ."

"What is a shopping mall?"

She caught her breath as Erin described the enclosed space with hundreds of shops and restaurants.

"And we go to events," Erin went on, "like football games and rock concerts."

"I have never been to a rock concert," Karina confessed. "The famous people, they do not come to such a small country as Baldavia. But I have records. Do you like the singing group, New Kids on the Block?"

"I know a girl back home who met those guys after a concert," Megan announced.

Karina clasped her hands. "Oh, it is true! In America, anything is possible!"

Carolyn came into the cabin. "Karina, here you are! Your coach has been looking for you. I think she's expecting you to meet her at the gym."

She went into her room, and Karina groaned. "Oh, no. I forgot my private practice session. The coach will be very angry." She got up from the bed. "I must go now."

Megan glanced out the window. It had started

to drizzle, and the girls wouldn't be able to do any of their outdoor activities. "Could we come with you?" she asked Karina. "It would be fun to watch."

Karina brightened. "Yes, please come. Perhaps she will not yell at me so much if you are there."

The girls started out of the cabin. Trina paused. "Megan, we *have* to ask Carolyn," she said quietly. "We can't just run off without letting her know where we're going."

Megan nodded. She practically pushed Karina out the door so she wouldn't see Trina asking permission.

The coach did not look at all pleased when they arrived. She spoke to Karina in Baldavian, which the girls couldn't understand, but her tone made her feelings clear. Then she spoke to the campers in English.

"You may sit and observe Karina's practice," she said. She paused, and then she spoke again. "You have all been most kind to Karina. But her purpose here is to practice and work at her gymnastics. Also, she must conserve her energy. Remember that she is an athlete, and she is in training for an important competition, where she can bring great honor to her country."

Karina looked like she was about to die of embarrassment. Meekly, the girls sat down to watch.

Karina wasn't quite as good as the first time they saw her perform. She wobbled on the balance beam, and when she went over the vault, she tripped on her landing. She's probably tired, Megan thought. After all, they'd been running around a lot the past couple of days.

The coach's expression was grim. She spoke harshly to the gymnast, and made her do the same thing over and over. Karina was looking miserable.

The coach left her to get some water from the cooler at the back of the gym. Karina hurried over to the bleachers where the girls were sitting.

"She wants me to work more. She says I am performing very badly."

"It happens to everyone sometimes," Megan said. "There are days when my tennis game is terrible."

Karina wasn't listening. "She is so mean! I am so . . . so . . ." She couldn't seem to find the word she was searching for, but it didn't matter. They could all see how mad she was.

It dawned on Megan that Karina wasn't as concerned about her performance as she was about the coach's attitude. She felt so sorry for her, having to put up with that demanding woman. Impulsively, Megan leaned forward. "Listen. Can you sneak out of your cabin tonight?"

"Sneak out?"

"Yes. Erin got a big box of goodies from home."

"Goodies? What are goodies?"

"Food!" Erin explained. "And I always get great stuff. We're going to have a midnight feast tonight in the cabin."

"Can you come?" Megan asked.

The coach was returning. Hastily, Karina said, "I will try." She hurried back to the beam.

Trina's face showed concern as she turned to Megan. "Do you think that was such a good idea?"

"Why?" Megan asked.

"You heard what the coach said. She's in training. She needs to rest."

Sarah seemed bothered too. "And the stuff Erin always gets in her goodie boxes—I don't think Karina's supposed to eat that kind of food if she's in training."

Megan had been in training herself, for tennis tournaments. She knew Sarah was right. But Karina looked so depressed! "She needs fun too," she argued. "It doesn't sound like she has much fun at home."

Erin agreed. "And the way that coach spoke to us when we came in . . . I don't think she's going to let Karina hang out with us anymore during the day."

Katie was on Megan's side too. "Karina wants to come. Did you see how her face lit up when she heard about the feast? She's going to be leaving here in just a few more days. We need to give her one more really terrific Sunnyside experience."

"Absolutely!" Megan said. She turned to watch Karina on the parallel bars. She was trying to swing over the upper bars, but she didn't have enough strength. She fell to the ground.

She wasn't hurt. But she didn't seem upset either. In fact, in Megan's eyes, she looked almost like she didn't care.

Chapter 6

"What time is it?" Megan asked.

"Exactly midnight," Sarah said. "And don't talk so loud. You don't want Carolyn to wake up."

Megan went to the window and peered out. "I don't see her coming."

"Of course you don't," Katie scoffed. "It's too dark out there to see anything."

"I was afraid of this," Megan sighed. "After what that mean coach said to us. She's probably locked the gymnasts in their cabin. Karina's going to be stuck with her and those creepy girls for the rest of the week."

"How can you be so sure the other girls are creepy?" Trina asked. "We haven't even met any of the other ones."

"Trina, you heard what Karina told us about them," Megan noted.

Katie laughed. "Hey, that's nothing compared to what we've all said about each other at one time or another."

Trina was shocked. "Not me!"

Sarah patted her shoulder. "No, you're too sweet. But when girls are cooped up together, they start getting on each other's nerves. Remember when you and I were sharing a bedroom at home? We didn't always get along."

"I'll bet it's the same for boys, too," Erin mused.

"You're right," Katie said. "You should hear my twin brothers fight!"

Trina nodded. "Yeah, I'll bet those Baldavian girls are actually friends in the long run."

"Let's open Erin's goodie box," Sarah suggested. "I'm starving."

Trina spread a blanket on the floor. Erin pulled the box out from under her bed. She untied the string, broke the tape, and opened it.

"What did you get?" Katie asked eagerly.

"Let's see . . ." Erin pulled out a white box and looked inside. "Mmm, I know what this is—chocolate chip cake with white chocolate frosting. There's a bag of butterscotch brownies, and oatmeal cookies, and homemade cheese sticks, and . . . ooh, pistachios, and caramel popcorn . . ."

"I'm in heaven," Sarah moaned.

There was a light rap on the door. Megan ran to open it before the knock woke Carolyn. "Karina! You made it!"

Karina's face was flushed and her eyes were bright with excitement as Megan hustled her inside.

"Did you have a hard time getting out of your cabin?" Katie asked.

"It was not easy," Karina said. "Two of the girls were talking very late, after the lights were out. I feared they would never go to sleep! The coach was in the separate room, but the door was open. I did not want to make any noise. So I removed my shoes. And then—I was so excited and nervous, I forgot to carry them out with me!"

Sure enough, Karina's feet were bare. They were wet, from the ground, and blades of grass clung to them.

"You'll catch a cold," Trina scolded mildly. She ran to the bathroom and returned with a towel. As Karina dried her feet, she smiled at them all.

"You are all so kind to invite me here! It is very strange. I have known you all such a short time, but I feel already we are very good friends."

70

"We feel the same about you," Trina said.

"I have been able to share my feelings with you so easily," Karina went on. "And of course, I feel I know you well because you have told me so much about your lives."

Megan was aware of an odd, unsettled feeling in her stomach. She didn't think that they'd actually *lied* to Karina about their lives. But they'd certainly let her believe some things that weren't exactly the absolute truth. Good friends didn't do that. Still, what did it matter? Karina would be leaving soon, and she'd never be the wiser. It was better that she carry great memories back to Baldavia, and leave this country believing everything in America was perfect and wonderful.

"Will you get in a lot of trouble if the coach finds out you're gone?" Trina asked anxiously.

Karina shrugged. "I do not care."

"Come sit on the blanket," Megan said.

Karina's eyes grew huge with rapture when she saw all the food spread out. "This is everything we are forbidden to eat!" she cried out.

Trina smiled, but she put a finger to her lips. "We have to keep our voices down so we don't wake Carolyn."

Karina raised her eyebrows. "But you said you girls can do anything you want."

71

"Oh, we can," Megan assured her. "But . . . um, we don't want to disturb her sleep. How was the rest of your practice, after we left?"

Karina's mouth was stuffed with brownies, so it was a minute before she was able to speak. "Terrible! I could do nothing right."

"Are you worried about that?" Katie asked.

"No. I believe I am beginning to hate gymnastics."

Sarah was puzzled. "But you must be looking forward to performing in the One World Games. You want Baldavia to win, don't you?"

Karina reached for a cookie. "I do not care anymore. I am tired of practice, and yelling, and taking orders. I do not want to work so hard anymore."

Trina turned sympathetic eyes on her. "You've just had a bad day. I'm sure all athletes go through feelings like that once in a while. Right, Megan?"

"Sure," Megan agreed. "There are days when I want to break my tennis racket over a coach's head! You'll feel better about this tomorrow."

But Karina shook her head vehemently. "No, I will not. It will be the same tomorrow."

"Do your teammates have the same feelings?" Sarah asked.

"I do not know," Karina replied. "I cannot

speak with them about this. When I am good at practice, I believe they are as you say, jealous. When I am not good, they become angry. When we do speak to each other, we quarrel." Her eyes became sad. "It is not like it is here. You are always friendly and happy to be with each other. You never have angry words."

Megan couldn't even bring herself to look at the others. Right that minute, they were all probably remembering some of the major battles they'd had right here in cabin six. There were times when they'd practically been at each other's throats.

And Karina thought they were always the best of friends. Boy, had they put on a good show for her!

Karina wolfed down a few more cookies, accepted a slice of cake, and continued. "Everything here is so wonderful. And from your stories, I can see that you have fun all the time, not just here at Camp Sunnyside. Your life is so much nicer than my life back in Baldavia."

Trina bit her lip. "You only think that because this is all new to you."

"Not so new," Karina said. "I have seen movies of life in America. The people wearing elegant clothes, going to fancy places, it is so glamorous. I used to believe this was just make-believe. But, listening to your stories, I can see now that it is true."

Trina opened her mouth. "But, Karina . . ." She got no further. Suddenly, there was a loud knocking at the door. Megan cast a frightened look at Carolyn's room. Katie leaped up and run to the door.

Katie barely had time to step aside before the gymnastics coach strode in. Her lips were pressed tightly together and her eyes were blazing. When she saw Karina, her face turned purple with rage.

"Oh no," Megan breathed, and clutched Sarah's hand.

In her own language, the coach barked something at Karina. Slowly, Karina got up. Megan could see Karina's hands shaking. But she spoke loudly and firmly.

In response, the coach's voice rose. So did Karina's. Then the coach saw the food on the blanket, and if possible, her voice got even louder.

Carolyn's door flew open. "What's going on here?" she cried out.

The coach turned to her, and spoke in English. "I discovered that Karina was missing from our cabin. I have found her here! Not only is she out after hours. She is breaking her training!" For the first time, she noticed Karina's feet. "And you have no shoes on! Karina, you are a gymnast! Your feet are very valuable!"

Carolyn leaned against the wall. "Oh, girls," she groaned. "What have you done?"

"Yes, your girls were wrong to lure her here," the coach snapped. "But I will not put the entire blame on them. Karina has been irresponsible. We will return to our cabin immediately, Karina!"

Karina drew herself up stiffly. "No."

The coach gasped, and stared at her in utter disbelief. "What did you say?"

"I said no. I will not return to the cabin. I am staying here."

Obviously, the coach was not accustomed to being disobeyed. For a second, she was speechless. "Karina, if you do not do as I say, you will be removed from the team."

The threat didn't seem to bother Karina. "Good. I wish to be removed from the team."

"Karina!" Megan cried out. But one sharp look from Carolyn made her clamp her mouth shut.

The coach appeared to be stunned. "Karina, if you leave the team, you will be sent back to Baldavia tomorrow."

75

"No, I am not returning to Baldavia," Karina said. "Not tomorrow, not ever."

The coach's voice dropped to whisper. "Karina, what are you saying?"

There was only the slightest tremble in Karina's voice. "I have seen a better world. I want the freedom to be as these girls are, to live my life as they do. I want to do what I want, whenever I want to do it." She paused for a deep breath before she continued.

"I have decided to defect. I will live in America."

Chapter 7

Megan woke up early the next morning. Sitting up, she pulled her knees to her chest and wrapped her arms around them. The cabin was silent, except for the soft, even breathing of the sleeping girls. The breathing seemed a little louder than usual. Maybe because there was one more person than usual sleeping there.

Megan leaned over to get a good look at the new resident of cabin six. Karina was curled up in Katie's sleeping bag on the floor. Seeing her there, looking so peaceful, it was hard for Megan to believe that the scene the night before had really taken place.

But it definitely happened. In her mind, Megan could still see the expression on the coach's face when Karina made her astounding announcement. She had never seen anyone look so shocked before.

And she could see Carolyn, with tousled hair and sleepy eyes, standing in the doorway, totally bewildered. Strangely enough, though, Carolyn didn't get terribly upset. She beckoned the coach into her room, and they stayed in there for a while. The girls couldn't hear what was being said.

When the coach emerged, she was calmer. She told Karina that her suitcase would be brought to her the next day. And then she left. Carolyn told the girls to put the food away and go to bed. And that was it.

Now, watching Karina, Megan wondered how she was able to sleep so easily. If *she* had just decided never to return to her home, to stay in a foreign country, she'd be up all night, chewing her nails and wondering if she'd made the right decision. But there was Karina, sound asleep, as if she didn't have a care in the world. She must feel awfully sure of herself, Megan thought.

It was kind of neat, in a way. Megan had wanted the Baldavians to have great feelings about Camp Sunnyside, the people, and America in general. She'd only been able to accomplish this with Karina. But obviously, her plans had been successful. A person had to really love a place to decide she wanted to live there forever!

Across the room, Katie stirred. She sat up, and looked at Megan. Her eyes shifted to Karina on the floor, then moved back to Megan. Seconds later, she climbed down from her bunk, crossed the room, and sat down on Megan's bed.

"Wild, huh?" Katie remarked. "She really wants to stay here in America."

"Guess we did a pretty good job, showing her how nice everything is here," Megan replied.

"No kidding. She's going to give up gymnastics, her family, her country . . . ," Katie whistled.

"Sh," Megan hissed. But Trina had already propped herself up on her elbows. She crawled out of bed and joined Megan and Katie on the bed.

"What do you think about this?" Katie asked in a whisper.

It was clear that Trina was troubled. "I'm worried about Karina."

"Me too," came a voice from above them. Sarah came down the ladder and plunked herself on Megan's bed.

"Why?" Megan asked. Then, with a sharp intake of breath, she asked, "Do you think the coach will try to kidnap her and force her back to Baldavia?"

"No," Trina said. "But have you ever thought about her future? What is she going to do here in America? She doesn't have any family here. Where will she live? She can't stay at Sunnyside forever."

"I wonder if she can even stay here for the rest of the summer," Sarah mused. "I don't think she has any money. And Sunnyside isn't free."

"You're telling me," Katie groaned. "My parents are always reminding me how expensive it is here."

That hadn't even occurred to Megan. "But if she just stays on the floor here, and doesn't take up a bunk, Ms. Winkle might let her stay for nothing. She wouldn't even have to have her own food. I never eat all of mine, and neither does Erin. We could share ours with her."

Trina wasn't satisfied. "But what about *after* Sunnyside? Where will she go then?"

Megan considered that. "Maybe one of our families can adopt her."

Sarah turned to Trina. "Can you imagine going to our parents and asking them if they'd mind another eleven-year-old daughter? I don't think either of them would jump for joy at the idea."

Megan couldn't imagine *her* parents being thrilled by the notion either. Katie, too, was shaking her head.

This is getting complicated, Megan thought. "What about Erin's parents? They can afford to have another kid living with them."

It seemed that even in her sleep, Erin knew when her name had come up in a conversation. Her eyes opened. Megan beckoned to her. Slowly, Erin rose, and practically tripped over Karina. She stared at the Baldavian girl, as if trying to remember who she was. Finally, she made her way to Megan's bed. "Is she going to stay here on the floor all summer?"

"Don't you want her here?" Megan asked.

Erin shrugged. "I don't care. She's okay."

"You want to take her home with you after the summer?" Megan asked hopefully.

Erin looked at her as if she'd lost her mind. *"What?"*

"Well, you're an only child, and . . ."

"And I plan to go on being an only child," Erin finished. "So don't get any bright ideas." She glanced over at Karina. "Now that she's staying, do we have to go on lying and acting happy all the time?"

Trina gave Megan a reproachful look. And Megan's stomach began to feel tense. What *was* Karina going to think when she realized they'd all been . . . well, not *lying* exactly, but exaggerating a little? Okay, a *lot*. How would she feel when she discovered that everything here wasn't always perfect and wonderful? And where would she go, what would she do? Megan couldn't help feeling sort of responsible. The cabin six girls had some serious thinking to do.

Now they were all silent, watching Karina on the floor. Karina turned over, rubbed her eyes, sat up and stretched. She beamed at the girls on the bed. "Oh, it is so wonderful to wake up here!"

The happiness on her face didn't help to erase Megan's concerns. "Let's get ready for breakfast," she said, hoping food would distract her from her thoughts.

But Sarah's next words put an end to that hope. "It's Monday."

"What is the problem?" Karina asked. "Why is Monday bad?"

"Oatmeal for breakfast," Sarah told her.

"Oatmeal," Karina repeated. "I am not sure what this is, oatmeal."

Megan didn't have the heart to explain. "Mondays aren't all bad," she said. "There's a bus to Pine Ridge this afternoon, and we can go if we want."

"That is where the other gymnasts went," Karina remembered. "They found it very nice."

"Oh, absolutely," Sarah said. "There's a bookstore, and a skating rink, a place where we can get the most fabulous hot fudge sundaes in the world."

"And shops," Erin added. That word put a special glow in her eyes.

"But I have no money for hot fudge sundaes," Karina said. "Or for anything else."

Trina gave Megan a pointed look. Megan bit her lip. "Well, maybe we can all chip in and buy you a sundae."

Carolyn came out of her room. "It's time for breakfast," she said briskly. She strode across the room to the bathroom.

"Isn't she going to say anything about last night?" Katie whispered in Megan's ear.

"Maybe she's forgotten about it," Megan replied.

"I doubt that," Katie said.

So did Megan. But they went to the dining hall with Carolyn, collected the dreaded oatmeal, sat down at their table, and Carolyn still didn't mention Karina's defection. Or the midnight feast, for that matter. It all seemed odd to

Megan. True, Carolyn wasn't as strict as some counselors, and she didn't dole out punishments for every infraction. But usually, when the girls broke a major rule, she scolded and lectured. Her silence was very strange. And she kept leaving the table, first to talk to Darrell, the swimming coach, then to Donna, the arts and crafts counselor.

The other Baldavians came into the dining hall. As they passed the cabin six table, two of them glanced at Karina, then quickly averted their eyes. One of them looked angry, the other seemed dazed. The coach didn't even glance in their direction.

"Karina, you haven't eaten your oatmeal," Carolyn said. "I thought you loved American food."

Karina eyed the gloppy mixture doubtfully. "I do not think this is typical American food," she replied. "We have this in Baldavia."

"And I'll bet the Baldavians don't like it any more than we do," Erin noted.

"This is correct," Karina said. "We ... I mean, they ... don't. But it is not important. I am certain that this will be the only thing I find here that is not wonderful." She sighed. "Everything else will be beautiful, and fun, and perfect."

As the girls headed back to cabin six after breakfast, Megan and Katie fell behind the others and talked privately. "Did you notice that Karina hasn't said a word about what she'll do after Sunnyside?" Katie asked.

Megan nodded. "Carolyn didn't say anything either. Why don't we talk to her about Karina? She might have some good ideas."

Katie agreed. Back in the cabin, Megan tossed the spread over her bed, and signaled to Katie. They went to Carolyn's door, rapped, and went in.

"We're worried about Karina," Megan said. "What's going to happen to her now?"

Carolyn was busily making her own bed. "I haven't the slightest idea," she replied.

Megan and Katie looked at each other in surprise. This wasn't like Carolyn at all. She was usually so concerned with all the girls.

"But Karina's not being very realistic," Katie said. "She doesn't know what life is really like here."

Carolyn finally faced them, and gazed at them evenly. "And whose fault is that?"

Megan and Katie had no answer to that.

"This is your problem, girls," Carolyn continued. "Yours and Karina's. I hope you work it out." Turning her back on them, she began hanging up some clothes.

Megan was dumbfounded, and from Katie's face she knew Katie's reaction was the same. They backed out of the room and closed the door.

There was a knock on the cabin door. Megan answered it. One of the Baldavian gymnasts was standing there, with a suitcase in her hand.

"Hi," Megan said. "Come in."

"No, thank you," the girl replied. "I have come to deliver this for Karina." She placed the suitcase down.

"Would you like me to get her?" Megan asked.

There was a tremble in the girl's voice as she said, "No." She turned away, but Megan said, "Wait, please. I want to ask you something."

"Yes?"

"Um, how do you all feel about Karina staying here?"

The girl looked down at the ground. When she lifted her head, Megan was startled to see tears in her eyes. "We are surprised. And we are saddened."

"Are you afraid you won't win the One World Games now?"

"There is that problem, of course. But it is more. We will miss her very much. As will her family." She shook her head sadly. "To leave Baldavia, our homeland—it is tragic. Karina has talked of nothing but America for days. But she has very strange ideas. America is nice, but Karina thinks it is like the movies. We have tried to tell her this is not true, but she will not listen."

That explained the arguing that Karina complained about, Megan thought.

"It is difficult to understand," the girl continued. "Where did she get these crazy ideas?"

Megan knew. Thanking the gymnast, she went back into the cabin. "Here's your suitcase, Karina."

Megan sat down on her bed. "Karina, have you thought about what you're going to do, or where you're going to live in America?"

"I will think of that later," Karina said. "I am certain everything will be all right. After all, as you said, in America anything is possible, yes?"

"That's what my grandfather always said," Sarah noted. "He called it the land of opportunity."

But not for eleven year olds on their own, Megan thought.

"Excuse me," Karina said. She went into the bathroom.

Sarah broke the silence. "Well, we wanted her to like it here."

"And we did a good job," Erin said.

"Yes," Megan sighed. "Too good. Guys, what are we going to do?"

There was no opportunity to discuss it. Karina returned from the bathroom. At the same time, Carolyn came out for inspection. This time, she didn't just breeze through the cabin. She paused at Katie's bed. "Katie, this bed is a mess! Redo it at once." She stopped at Megan's, too. "Megan, what's that towel doing on your bed post? It doesn't belong there."

Erin was scolded for leaving cosmetics all over her nightstand. And Sarah was criticized for not folding her pajamas and placing them under her pillow. She couldn't find anything wrong with Trina's bed, but Karina wasn't spared.

"Karina, I don't want to see that sleeping bag on the floor. Roll it up and put it away."

Megan could see that Karina was startled. She'd never seen Carolyn when the counselor was on the warpath.

But the biggest surprise was yet to come. "What time is the bus leaving for Pine Ridge?" Erin asked.

"It doesn't matter," Carolyn informed her. "None of you are going."

Six astonished girls were speechless. "Why not?" Megan got up the courage to ask.

"That little midnight feast last night has earned you five demerits," Carolyn announced. "You're all confined to the cabin from two o'clock till dinner." With that, she returned to her room and closed the door.

Karina turned to the other girls in dismay. "I do not understand. What are demerits?"

The girls tried to explain on the way to the swimming pool, but Karina was still confused. Megan couldn't blame her. After all, the girls had given her the impression that they could get away with anything.

It seemed to her that everyone was in a bad mood that day. At the pool, Darrell spoke to them sharply for being late. "Line up alongside the pool," he ordered. "We're going to work on diving today."

They formed a line. Darrell issued short blasts on his whistle, and at the sound, the girls dived one after another. When they all emerged from the water, he wasn't smiling. "That was pathetic!" he announced. "You're going to do it again. And you're going to keep on doing it until each and every one of you gets it right!"

"Can we not play with the frisbee today?" Karina asked Megan.

89

"No talking!" Darrell yelled.

The girls lined up again, and did their dives. Megan didn't think they looked so bad, but Darrell still wasn't satisfied. He made them do it again. And again. He didn't even let them have their usual fifteen minutes of free time at the end of the lesson. He kept them diving right to the end of the pool period.

"I did not enjoy that so much today," Karina told the others as they went back to the cabin to change. "Why could we not have fun?"

"It's not always fun here, Karina," Trina told her.

"But you said you always have fun," Karina said to Megan.

Megan managed a feeble smile. "Well, most of the time we do."

Karina frowned. "I hope we will be doing something fun in arts and crafts."

But it was not to be. When they entered the arts and crafts cabin, Donna had an announcement to make. "This place is a mess," she said. "You girls have not been cleaning up after yourselves. We are going to spend this period getting everything cleaned up and organized."

Washing paintbrushes was apparently not Karina's idea of fun. Megan watched her face get glummer and gloomier.

After arts and crafts, they stopped to pick up their mail. As they waited in line, Ms. Winkle came by. "Ah, Karina," she said. "I understand you have decided to stay with us here at Camp Sunnyside."

"That is true," Karina said. "This is such a beautiful place, and I believe . . ."

Ms. Winkle didn't let her finish. "I have told Carolyn to explain the camp rules and regulations to you. Learn them, and follow them." She walked away.

"She didn't even say *welcome*," Sarah murmured to Megan. "That didn't sound like Ms. Winkle at all!"

"What are these rules and regulations?" Karina asked.

"Oh, just the usual stuff," Megan said vaguely. They'd reached the front of the line. "Could I have the mail for cabin six, please?"

Erin and Megan both got letters, and so did Karina. Karina took one look at the envelope, and then stuck it in her pocket. "Aren't you going to read it?" Katie asked.

"It is from my parents," Karina said. "I do not wish to read it now."

"You know, you're going to have to write them and tell them you've decided to stay here," Trina said gently. Karina didn't say anything.

As they walked to the dining hall, Erin tore her letter open and started reading. Then she let out a moan.

"What's the matter?" Sarah asked.

"My parents got my class schedule for this fall. And I've got a witch for history."

"A witch!" Karina gasped. "You mean, like in the fairy tales, the evil one who casts spells?"

"Worse," Erin groaned. "This is the evil one who piles on the homework every day and makes you write essays and gives quizzes every week."

"But I thought you American girls didn't have to work very hard at school," Karina said.

Megan felt like a creep. "Well, sometimes, we do."

There wasn't much happiness waiting for them in the dining hall. Lunch was meat loaf, lumpy mashed potatoes, and plain, ordinary vanilla pudding for dessert. As Karina poked at her food, Megan could see that her opinion of American food was rapidly changing.

"Who's your letter from, Megan?" Sarah asked.

"My mom. She sent a photo." She passed around the picture of her mother, father, and baby brother.

When the picture reached Karina, her forehead puckered. "What is this place?"

"Our house," Megan said.

"It is not like the home of Erin."

Megan managed a grin. "No, it certainly isn't. But Erin's rich. We're just . . . well, we're not poor. But we're definitely not rich."

"It does not look so different from my home in Baldavia," Karina remarked.

Ms. Winkle got up to make some announcements. "The bus to Pine Ridge will be leaving immediately after lunch. Campers who plan to go should meet in front of the dining hall."

The cabin six girls turned to Carolyn with beseeching eyes. But Carolyn shook her head. "No way. You girls are spending the afternoon in the cabin."

The girls dragged their feet going back. Once inside, Megan planted her face at the window. "What crummy luck. The weather's fantastic, and we're stuck inside."

"Whose brilliant idea was it anyway, to have a midnight feast?" Katie asked.

"It's not my fault," Megan retorted. "Erin was the one who got the box of food."

"Are you blaming me for that?" Erin asked.

"Come on, you guys," Trina said. "We've had

93

these feasts before. We were just unlucky this time. We got caught at it."

"We wouldn't have gotten caught," Sarah muttered, "if that coach hadn't showed up and made so much noise."

Erin nodded. "And she wouldn't have come if you hadn't invited Karina, Megan."

Megan could see the hurt on Karina's face. "Don't blame her! It's not her fault!"

"It's nobody's fault," Trina said. "Or maybe it's all our faults. Anyway, there's nothing we can do about it now. Let's play a game or something. How about Scrabble?"

"Boring," Erin grumbled. She opened her bottle of nail polish remover.

"Ick, don't do that in here," Megan said. "That stuff stinks up the place."

"Too bad," Erin snapped back.

"Where's my book?" Sarah asked. "I left it right here on the nightstand."

"I'm using it to keep my nightstand from wobbling," Katie said.

Sarah went over to Katie's nightstand. There was her book, on the floor under one of the legs. Sarah reached down and pulled it out. The nightstand tipped, and everything on it fell off.

"Hey, what are you doing?" Katie yelled in outrage.

"Well, you shouldn't have taken my book without asking!" Sarah snapped back.

Karina was watching all this with alarm. "What is happening here? You never argue with each other. Why are you acting like this?"

Trina tried to comfort her. "I think we're just all in bad moods, Karina. It happens sometimes."

Karina sat down on Erin's bed. The motion made the polish remover bottle spill.

"Oh, no!" Erin wailed.

Karina jumped up. "I am sorry!"

"Oh, great," Sarah moaned. "Now this place is *really* going to stink."

Karina looked like she was about to burst into tears. "I do not understand! What is happening? Everything has been so perfect until today."

"No place is perfect all the time," Trina told her. "Not even Camp Sunnyside."

For once, Megan made no effort to contradict this. "Do you still want to stay here, Karina?"

Slowly, Karina nodded. "Yes, of course. I will stay."

But to Megan, Karina didn't sound anywhere near as sure of herself as she had the night before.

Chapter 8

It was a dreary scene in cabin six. The girls had stopped quarreling, but Megan thought the silence in the room was just as creepy. It wasn't as if they'd never bickered before, even worse than today. But today felt different.

Megan decided this was because of Karina. Right that minute, the Baldavian girl was sitting on Trina's bed, leafing through a magazine. Megan could tell she wasn't really reading it, though. Every few minutes, she'd gaze around the room, with a hurt and bewildered expression.

Carolyn came in. "Megan, would you run an errand for me, please?"

Megan would do anything to get out of that cabin. "Sure." She leaped off her bed.

"I want you to take this note to Ms. Winkle. And come right back."

"How come *she* gets to leave," Erin grumbled. Carolyn ignored her and went back to her room.

Free of that gloomy atmosphere, Megan took her time walking to Ms. Winkle's office. She gave the note to the director's secretary, and started back. Now she walked even more slowly. She was in no rush to get back to the cabin.

Passing the gym, she saw the Baldavians coming out. As they walked by, one of the gymnasts turned to her. "Americans," she muttered darkly.

Startled, Megan asked, "What did you say?"

"It is all your fault," the girl snapped. Then she burst into tears.

As the coach spoke to the girl softly, Megan realized all the gymnasts were giving her unhappy looks. Then the coach spoke to the group, and they began walking away. But the woman stayed behind, and spoke to Megan.

"I regret the rudeness of my girls," she said. "But they are very saddened at the loss of Karina."

Megan shifted her weight from one foot to the other. "Uh, well, I'm sure they'll do fine in the games anyway."

"That is not why they are sad. They care deeply for Karina, and they will miss her."

"Oh." Megan was finding it difficult to look

the woman in the face. "Well, I'm sorry. But I guess Karina knows what she wants to do."

"Does she?" The woman paused. Then she said, "I must tell you, this is the situation I feared. This is why I kept my gymnasts separated from the campers, and why I did not approve of your friendship with Karina."

Megan looked up. "I don't understand."

"My gymnasts must work very hard to become champions," the coach said. "It is difficult for them. I was afraid that when they saw the campers here, having fun, they would become envious, and unable to concentrate. They would want to join with you, and participate in your good times."

"Everyone needs some fun once in a while," Megan said. "Even gymnasts."

"Yes, of course. And they will have fun when the games are finished. But for now, discipline is essential. That is why it is necessary for me to be strict with my team. Particularly Karina."

Megan recalled the first time she saw Karina practice. "She's good, isn't she?"

"Yes, she is very talented, perhaps the most talented on the team. But sometimes she can be lazy." The coach sighed deeply. "I know that achieving the world championship would have made her very happy, and she would know that all her efforts were worthwhile. Baldavia would have been very proud of her. I fear she will regret this decision someday."

Megan's hands were getting sweaty. She rubbed them on her shorts. "Maybe she could be a gymnast in America."

"Maybe. But of course, there is more to her decision than that. To leave one's home, one's family, one's country—it is a very serious step. Someday, Karina will realize that she loved her country. But by then, it will be too late."

Strange. A second before, Megan had been sweating. Now she shivered. "Um, do you want me to give her any message?"

The coach placed a hand gently on her shoulder. "Yes. Tell her I miss her. Her teammates miss her. And all of Baldavia will miss her."

The coach walked away. Megan stared after her for a moment. Then she began running.

Bursting into the cabin, she looked around wildly. "Where's Karina?"

"She's in Carolyn's room," Trina said, nodding toward the closed door. "I think Carolyn's explaining the camp rules and regulations to her."

"What's the matter?" Sarah asked. "You look upset."

Megan reported her conversation with the

coach. "Guys, I think the coach is right. We've got to convince Karina to go back."

"But how?" Katie asked. "Here we're having this awful day, and she *still* wants to stay."

The door to Carolyn's room opened. Karina came out, and she didn't look very happy at all. "So many rules," she murmured.

"Girls, I'm letting you go now," Carolyn announced. "No more midnight feasts, okay?"

The girls nodded, though Megan suspected several sets of fingers were crossed behind some backs.

Carolyn checked her watch. "You've got about forty-five minutes until dinner. I'll see you in the dining hall."

"What do you guys want to do?" Trina asked.

"Let's take a walk," Megan suggested.

The idea didn't receive any wild enthusiasm, but the girls got up and followed her out. Megan linked her arm with Karina's, and walked ahead of the others.

"You look like something's bothering you," she said to Karina. "What's wrong?"

"Carolyn told me about the rules of Camp Sunnyside," Karina replied. "What we have to do, and wear, and how we have to behave. I am very confused! I believed you were free to do what you want here. That is what you told me."

It was confession time. Megan took a deep breath. "Karina, we wanted you to think everything here was wonderful. So you'd return to Baldavia with good feelings about America. I guess we sort of made everything sound better than it really is."

"Then you are not happy here?" Karina asked.

"Oh, sure, we're happy. Most of the time. But we're not free to do anything we want. Kids never are! Not even at Camp Sunnyside. Not even in America."

Karina's chin was set stubbornly. "But it is still more free for you, in America, than for me, in Baldavia."

"Karina, did I ever tell you about a typical day for me, at home?"

Karina shook her head. Megan began. "Well, I wake up. I eat breakfast. I go to school. I've got a teacher who makes us do our math problems over and over till we get them right. She's always scolding me for daydreaming, or talking, or passing notes. We have to march in single file everywhere we go. Lunch is absolutely disgusting. Sometimes we can't even figure out what we're eating!"

Karina was skeptical. "You are making up a story."

"No, I'm not. After school, I have a tennis lesson or a piano lesson, and I don't know who's meaner, the tennis coach or the piano teacher. I go home, and I do homework. This teacher I've got really piles it on. Doesn't this sound like your typical day in Baldavia?"

"But you have no chores," Karina pointed out. "You have servants to clean up."

"Servants!" Megan uttered a short laugh. "The only servant in our house is me! I have to make my bed, and help with the dishes, and all that. Plus, I have to help take care of my baby brother."

"But Erin said . . ."

"Erin's rich," Megan interrupted. "She's the only one who has a maid, and her own TV, and all that stuff. Erin is *not* a typical American girl." She looked at Karina carefully. Was she getting through to her?

They were walking by the gym. Trina caught up with Megan and Karina. "Could we go in here for a little while?"

"Why?" Karina asked.

Trina gave her a self-conscious smile. "Well, I was wondering if you could give me some help. You see, I do some gymnastics. But I'm terrible on the balance beam. Maybe you could give me some pointers, show me what I'm doing wrong."

"Yes, I will be glad to do that," Karina said.

The gym was empty. Karina and Trina went to the balance beam, while the others sat on the bleachers to watch. Trina got on the beam and showed Karina what she could do.

"You are not using your arms properly," Karina said. "That is why you have difficulty with your balance. And you must keep your knees locked. That will give you a better line."

Trina jumped off. "Could you demonstrate for me?"

Karina mounted the beam. The girls watched as she moved gracefully from one end to the middle, executed a perfect split, rose, did a somersault, and then walked on her hands. Her dismount included a perfect flip in the air. In the middle of the flip, Megan saw something fly out of her pocket.

"That was wonderful!" Trina exclaimed. "Oh, Karina, you're so talented! How can you give this up?"

Meanwhile, Megan had retrieved the object that fell out of Karina's pocket. It was her unopened letter. "Here," she said, handing it to Karina.

Karina stared at the envelope. "Why don't you read it?" Trina asked softly. "We'd like to hear what's going on in Baldavia."

Karina ripped it open. The girls watched silently as she read. "Look," Katie whispered to Megan. "She's crying."

Sure enough, a tear was trickling down Karina's face. "Is it bad news?" Trina asked anxiously.

"No," Karina said. "My mother says . . . she says they are very proud of me. She says my sister has invited friends to watch the gymnastics meet on television next week. She says . . ." here, she choked up. Her voice trembled. "She says they love me and they miss me very much, and there will be a big celebration when I return home."

"Gee," Erin said. "Sounds like fun. Too bad you're going to miss it."

Karina stuffed the letter back into her pocket. Trina put an arm around her. "Come on, it's time for dinner."

"It's macaroni and cheese tonight," Sarah added. "That's a Camp Sunnyside specialty!"

But for the first time, Karina didn't seem interested in food. She was quiet all the way to the dining hall. They got their food, joined Carolyn at their table, and began to eat.

Megan toyed with her macaroni and cheese. It was one of her favorite meals, but she had no appetite. She noticed that Karina wasn't eating much either.

Ms. Winkle was making her announcements. "We have a special treat in store for us, campers. The Baldavian gymnastics team has kindly offered to give us an exhibition of their talents. The program will take place tonight, at eight o'clock, in the gymnasium."

"Oh, wow," Trina said. "I can't wait to see this!"

"Finally, something good is happening today," Erin commented. The others echoed the enthusiasm. But Megan couldn't help noticing that one person at their table didn't look particularly ecstatic about this news at all.

"It's time to go the gym," Carolyn said.

The girls were all ready, identically dressed in fresh Sunnyside tee shirts and shorts. They started for the door.

Only Karina remained seated on Trina's bed. "Come on, Karina," Megan said. "We don't want to be late."

"I do not wish to go," Karina said. "I will stay here."

Carolyn spoke kindly but firmly. "I'm afraid I can't allow that, Karina. That's one of the Camp Sunnyside rules that I told you about, remember? Campers are not allowed to stay alone in a cabin without a counselor."

"Then, could you please stay here with me?" Karina asked plaintively.

"No," Carolyn said. "I'm sorry, dear, but I want to see the gymnasts."

Reluctantly, Karina rose and joined the others. She dragged her feet, walking behind the others all the way to the gym. Megan tried talking to her, but Karina didn't seem to be in the mood for any conversation.

The bleachers were packed with campers, chattering excitedly in anticipation of the event. The cabin six girls took their seats, and watched expectantly as Ms. Winkle went to the microphone at the end of the room.

"I'm sure I speak for you all when I say that we are pleased and honored to have had the Baldavian championship gymnastics team with us. Tomorrow, they leave to compete in the One World Games, and we wish them success. Tonight, we have the opportunity to see what they'll be doing at the games. Let's have a nice round of applause for the Baldavian gymnasts!"

The Sunnyside girls cheered and clapped as the seven members of the team marched out onto the floor. "Hey, those are cool uniforms," Erin said.

"Blue and gold," Karina murmured. "They are the colors of the flag of Baldavia."

The gymnasts took seats on the bottom row of the bleachers. One remained standing. She took off the jacket that covered her leotard, and proceeded to the balance beam.

"That is Lydia," Karina said quietly.

Megan watched Lydia's routine with interest. "Wow, she's really good," she said to Trina.

Trina nodded. "But not as good as Karina, I think."

Megan agreed. Furtively, she glanced at Karina. Karina's eyes were glassy as she watched the performance. What was going on in her head, Megan wondered. Was she having doubts about her decision to stay?

Then she noticed two of the gymnasts making their way up the bleachers. They stopped when they reached the level where the cabin six group was sitting.

"Karina," one of them said. She began speaking in Baldavian. The other handed Karina something wrapped in tissue paper. They both leaned toward her. One at a time, they kissed her on both cheeks. Then they went back down the bleachers.

"What was that all about?" Megan asked Karina.

"They wanted to say good-bye," Karina reported dully. "And to give me something to remember them by. A . . . what do you call it? Oh yes. A souvenir."

She unwrapped the package. Under the tissue lay a blue and gold leotard and jacket. "My uniform," she whispered.

"That's nice," Megan said.

Karina stared straight ahead. Another gymnast had begun her floor routine on the mat. "Natalia," Karina whispered.

Megan turned to watch Natalia. The girl struck a pose, and some music began playing. She began a series of somersaults, one after another, moving so fast that she became a blur. Her leaps were so high, and she stayed in the air so long, she made it seem as if gravity didn't exist.

Megan couldn't take her eyes off Natalia. It was a long demonstration, but the girl never seemed to run out of energy. Every movement she made looked perfect to Megan. All eyes were glued to her, and the entire gymnasium was totally silent as the performance went on.

Natalia finished up with an incredible series of flips. The audience applauded wildly.

"She's amazing!" Katie cried out.

"Unbelievable!" Trina exclaimed.

"Fantastic," Megan echoed, watching the girl take a bow. "What did you think, Karina?"

When there was no response, she turned. The seat next to her was empty. "Where did Karina go?" she asked the others.

No one knew. And then Erin yelled, "Look!" She pointed.

Megan gasped. There on the gymnasium floor, dressed in blue and gold, leaping onto the parallel bars, was Karina.

Chapter 9

"Hurry up!" Megan yelled to her cabin mates the next morning. "Or we'll miss them!"

She tapped her foot impatiently as the others hurriedly tied shoelaces and tucked their shirts into their shorts. Carolyn came out of her room and joined them. Then they all ran out of the cabin. Megan raced ahead, but she could hear the others close behind.

They reached Ms. Winkle's office, and Megan paused to catch her breath. She heaved a sigh of relief. They weren't too late. The bus was still there.

Other campers had gathered to say good-bye to the Baldavian gymnasts. And there were some strangers, too. "Look, a television camera," Katie pointed out.

Erin moaned. "Oh, no, and my hair's a mess!

110

Megan was rushing me so much I didn't have time to dry it."

Sarah rolled her eyes. "I don't think anyone's going to be pointing the camera at you, Erin."

"Why are television people here?" Megan wondered

"I think I know why," Carolyn said. "There was an article in the newspaper yesterday that said the Baldavians are the favorites for a gold medal. That's a big deal, since this is the first year Baldavia has sent a team to the games."

Megan was hopping up and down with excitement. "Wouldn't that be incredibly neat, if they win? We can tell our families that we actually know a member of the team."

Trina nodded. "I'm glad we won't be saying we know someone who *used* to be on the team."

Sarah agreed. "I'm going to miss Karina. But I'm glad she decided to leave." She grinned. "I'll never forget that look on Megan's face when she saw Karina on the gym floor last night! You were stunned, Megan!"

"But I was glad, too," Megan said. Something occurred to her. "Carolyn, is that why you were acting so mean yesterday? To make Karina want to leave?"

Carolyn gave her a look of wide-eyed innocence. "Mean? *Me?*" But her lips were twitching.

"And I'll bet you told Darrell and Donna to act mean too," Katie said.

Now Carolyn was actually grinning. "Just don't get any ideas about another midnight feast. Remember, I don't need a Baldavian gymnast for an excuse to get tough!"

"Here they come!" Megan yelled. Ms. Winkle's door opened, and the gymnasts came out, followed by their coach. A cheer went up from the crowd, and someone yelled, "Go for the gold, Baldavia!"

The gymnasts mingled with the crowd, shaking hands. Some of the campers asked for their autographs. Karina hurried over to the cabin six group. One by one, each of the campers hugged her.

"I will miss you all," Karina said. "Now you must come to Baldavia to visit me."

"Here," Megan said, handing her a piece of paper. "We all wrote down our home addresses for you."

Karina must have had the same idea. She passed around papers. "This is my address. We will write to each other, yes?"

"Absolutely," Megan promised. She was pleased with the idea, feeling pretty sure she'd be the only girl in her hometown with a Baldavian pen pal.

"Megan, I have something to return to you," Karina said. She held out a Camp Sunnyside tee shirt.

But Megan wouldn't accept it. "Keep it. You should have a souvenir, so you won't forget us."

"I will never forget my American friends," Karina stated. She gave Megan another hug, and whispered, "especially you."

The Baldavian coach appeared behind her. For once, her face wasn't stern at all. She smiled at Megan, and her lips moved. With all the noise around them, Megan couldn't actually hear her. But it was clear that what the coach had said was, "Thank you."

Megan smiled back at her. She didn't really feel like she could take the credit for Karina's change of heart. If anything, she should be blamed for causing the problem in the first place. Well, everything had worked out okay in the end, so there was no point in thinking about what might have been. But she'd learned her lesson. If Camp Sunnyside ever had any more foreign visitors, she'd let them learn to love America on their own!

"We'll be watching you in the games on television," Trina told Karina. "And we'll be rooting for you."

"Bet you win a gold medal," Katie said.

Karina smiled modestly. "Oh, I'd be happy with a silver one, or a bronze."

"Go for the gold," Erin advised her. "Gold is much more valuable than silver or bronze." Then she stepped back and clutched her head. "Oh no, here comes the television camera."

But just as Sarah had said, it wasn't pointed at her. The woman holding the camera aimed it in Karina's direction, and a man with a microphone approached her. He spoke in the direction of the camera. "We are here at Camp Sunnyside, talking to the members of the gymnastics team from Baldavia, on their way to the One World Games." Then he turned to Karina.

"Is this your first trip to America, young lady?" He extended the microphone toward her.

"Yes, it is," Karina told him.

"What do you think of this country? Are you enjoying your visit?"

"Yes, I am enjoying it very much," Karina replied. "I am learning many things about this wonderful country."

"Tell us what you've learned," the man said.

Karina cocked her head thoughtfully. "I have learned that the people are very kind and generous. I learned that the food ... *some* of the food is delicious. And many other things."

"What's the most important thing you've learned?"

Karina smiled. She turned slightly and winked at Megan. Then she looked back into the camera and answered the question.

"America is really not so different from Baldavia!"

MEET THE GIRLS FROM CABIN SIX IN

(#17) CAMP SPAGHETTI   76556-X ($3.50 US/$4.25 Can)

(#16) HAPPILY EVER AFTER   76555-1 ($3.50 US/$4.25 Can)

(#15) CHRISTMAS BREAK   76553-5 ($2.99 US/$3.50 Can)

(#14) MEGAN'S GHOST   76552-7 ($2.99 US/$3.50 Can)

(#13) BIG SISTER BLUES   76551-9 ($2.95 US/$3.50 Can)

(#12) THE TENNIS TRAP   76184-X ($2.95 US/$3.50 Can)

(#11) THE PROBLEM WITH PARENTS
   76183-1 ($2.95 US/$3.50 Can)

(#10) ERIN AND THE MOVIE STAR   76181-5 ($2.95 US/$3.50 Can)

(#9) THE NEW-AND-IMPROVED SARAH
   76180-7 ($2.95 US/$3.50 Can)

(#8) TOO MANY COUNSELORS   75913-6 ($2.95 US/$3.50 Can)

(#7) A WITCH IN CABIN SIX   75912-8 ($2.95 US/$3.50 Can)

(#6) KATIE STEALS THE SHOW   75910-1 ($2.95 US/$3.50 Can)

(#5) LOOKING FOR TROUBLE   75909-8 ($2.95 US/$3.50 Can)

(#4) NEW GIRL IN CABIN SIX   75703-6 ($2.95 US/$3.50 Can)

(#3) COLOR WAR!   75702-8 ($3.50 US/$4.25 Can)

(#2) CABIN SIX PLAYS CUPID   75701-X ($2.95 US/$3.50 Can)

(#1) NO BOYS ALLOWED!   75700-1 ($2.95 US/$3.50 Can)

Buy these books at your local bookstore or use this coupon for ordering:
....
Mail to: Avon Books, Dept BP, Box 767, Rte 2, Dresden, TN 38225   B
Please send me the book(s) I have checked above.
☐ My check or money order—no cash or CODs please—for $_____ is enclosed
(please add $1.50 to cover postage and handling for each book ordered—Canadian
residents add 7% GST).
☐ Charge my VISA/MC Acct#_____ Exp Date _____
Phone No _____ Minimum credit card order is $6.00 (please add postage
and handling charge of $2.00 plus 50 cents per title after the first two books to a maximum
of six dollars—Canadian residents add 7% GST). For faster service, call 1-800-762-0779.
Residents of Tennessee, please call 1-800-633-1607. Prices and numbers are subject to
change without notice. Please allow six to eight weeks for delivery.

Name_____

Address_____

City _____ State/Zip _____

SUN 0392

Celebrating 40 Years of Cleary Kids!

CAMELOT presents
CLEARY FAVORITES!

- **HENRY HUGGINS**
  70912-0 ($3.50 US/$4.25 Can)
- **HENRY AND BEEZUS**
  70914-7 ($3.50 US/$4.25 Can)
- **HENRY AND THE CLUBHOUSE**
  70915-5 ($3.50 US/$4.25 Can)
- **ELLEN TEBBITS**
  70913-9 ($3.50 US/$4.25 Can)
- **HENRY AND RIBSY**
  70917-1 ($3.50 US/$4.25 Can)
- **BEEZUS AND RAMONA**
  70918-X ($3.50 US/$4.25 Can)
- **RAMONA AND HER FATHER**
  70916-3 ($3.50 US/$4.25 Can)
- **MITCH AND AMY**
  70925-2 ($3.50 US/$4.25 Can)
- **RUNAWAY RALPH**
  70953-8 ($3.50 US/$4.25 Can)

- **HENRY AND THE PAPER ROUTE**
  70921-X ($3.50 US/$4.25 Can)
- **RAMONA AND HER MOTHER**
  70952-X ($3.50 US/$4.25 Can)
- **OTIS SPOFFORD**
  70919-8 ($3.50 US/$4.25 Can)
- **THE MOUSE AND THE MOTORCYCLE**
  70924-4 ($3.50 US/$4.25 Can)
- **SOCKS**
  70926-0 ($3.50 US/$4.25 Can)
- **EMILY'S RUNAWAY IMAGINATION**
  70923-6 ($3.50 US/$4.25 Can)
- **MUGGIE MAGGIE**
  71087-0 ($3.50 US/$4.25 Can)
- **RAMONA THE PEST**
  70954-6 ($3.50 US/$4.25 Can)

Buy these books at your local bookstore or use this coupon for ordering:
....
Mail to: Avon Books, Dept BP, Box 767, Rte 2, Dresden, TN 38225   B
Please send me the book(s) I have checked above.
□ My check or money order—no cash or CODs please—for $_____ is enclosed
(please add $1.50 to cover postage and handling for each book ordered—Canadian
residents add 7% GST).
□ Charge my VISA/MC Acct# _____ Exp Date _____
Phone No _____ Minimum credit card order is $6.00 (please add postage
and handling charge of $2.00 plus 50 cents per title after the first two books to a maximum
of six dollars—Canadian residents add 7% GST). For faster service, call 1-800-762-0779.
Residents of Tennessee, please call 1-800-633-1607. Prices and numbers are subject to
change without notice. Please allow six to eight weeks for delivery.

Name _____

Address _____

City _____ State/Zip _____

BEV 0392

WORLDS OF WONDER
FROM
AVON CAMELOT

THE INDIAN IN THE CUPBOARD
60012-9/$3.25US/$3.95Can

THE RETURN OF THE INDIAN
70284-3/$3.50US only

Lynne Reid Banks

"Banks conjures up a story that is both thoughtful and captivating and interweaves the fantasy with care and believability" *Booklist*

THE HUNKY-DORY DAIRY
Anne Lindbergh   70320-3/$2.95US/$3.75Can

"A beguiling fantasy...full of warmth, wit and charm"
Kirkus Reviews

THE MAGIC OF THE GLITS
C.S. Adler   70403-X/$2.50US/$3.25Can

"A truly magical book" *The Reading Teacher*

GOOD-BYE PINK PIG
C.S. Adler   70175-8/$2.75US/$3.25 Can

Every fifth grader needs a friend she can count on!

Buy these books at your local bookstore or use this coupon for ordering:

Mail to: Avon Books, Dept BP, Box 767, Rte 2, Dresden, TN 38225   B
Please send me the book(s) I have checked above.
☐ My check or money order—no cash or CODs please—for $_____ is enclosed
(please add $1.50 to cover postage and handling for each book ordered—Canadian
residents add 7% GST).
☐ Charge my VISA/MC Acct#_____ Exp Date _____
Phone No _____ Minimum credit card order is $6.00 (please add postage
and handling charge of $2.00 plus 50 cents per title after the first two books to a maximum
of six dollars—Canadian residents add 7% GST). For faster service, call 1-800-762-0779.
Residents of Tennessee, please call 1-800-633-1607. Prices and numbers are subject to
change without notice. Please allow six to eight weeks for delivery.

Name_____

Address _____

City _____ State/Zip _____

WON   0391

Fifth-grade fun from

BEATRICE GORMLEY

MORE FIFTH GRADE MAGIC 70883-3/$3.50/$4.25
When Amy uses her magic calendar to make her
wishes come true, things get out of control.

THE MAGIC MEAN MACHINE 75519-X/$2.95/$3.50
Alison Harrity can't beat Spencer at chess until
scientific genius Marvin helps her.

FIFTH-GRADE MAGIC   67439-1/$2.95/$3.50
Fifth-grader Gretchen Nichols would do anything to
have the lead in the school play—even believe in
magic!

And don't miss
THE GHASTLY GLASSES   70262-2/$2.95/$3.50
BEST FRIEND INSURANCE   69854-4/$2.50/$2.95
PAUL'S VOLCANO   70562-1/$2.50/$3.25

Buy these books at your local bookstore or use this coupon for ordering:

Mail to: Avon Books, Dept BP, Box 767, Rte 2, Dresden, TN 38225   B
Please send me the book(s) I have checked above.
☐ My check or money order—no cash or CODs please—for $_____ is enclosed
(please add $1.50 to cover postage and handling for each book ordered—Canadian
residents add 7% GST).
☐ Charge my VISA/MC Acct#_____ Exp Date_____
Phone No_____Minimum credit card order is $6.00 (please add postage
and handling charge of $2.00 plus 50 cents per title after the first two books to a maximum
of six dollars—Canadian residents add 7% GST). For faster service, call 1-800-762-0779.
Residents of Tennessee, please call 1-800-633-1607. Prices and numbers are subject to
change without notice. Please allow six to eight weeks for delivery.

Name_____

Address_____

City_____ State/Zip_____

GOR 1291